What We Deserved:
Stories from a New York Life

What We Deserved:
Stories from a New York Life

Steven Schrader

Hanging Loose Press
Brooklyn, New York

Published by Hanging Loose Press, 231 Wyckoff Street, Brooklyn, NY 11217-2208. All rights reserved. No part of this book may be reproduced without the publisher's written permission, except for brief quotations in reviews.

Hanging Loose thanks the Literature Program of New York State Council on the arts for a grant in support of the publication of this book.

www.hangingloosepress.com

Printed in the United States of America
10 9 8 7 6 5 4 3 2 1

Cover art: "Snow Below Columbus Circle" pastel, 27 $^1/_2$ x 16 $^1/_2$", 1987 by Louise Hamlin
Cover design by Benjamin Piekut

Acknowledgments: A number of these stories have appeared in *Hanging Loose* magazine. "Tomek and Julia" appeared in *Transfer* magazine. "First Days of Divorce" was published in the book *On Sundays We Visit the In-Laws*.

I'd like to thank Glenda Adams and Bill Zavatsky for their careful readings of my manuscript and their many helpful suggestions. For their support and encouragement I would also like to thank Anne Brashler, Carol Conroy, Elaine Edelman, Phyllis Raphael, Louise Rose, and Roger Wall. And, finally I'd like to thank Dick Lourie at Hanging Loose for his sympathetic and invaluable editing, and also the rest of the folks at Hanging Loose: Donna Brook, Marie Carter, Bob Hershon, and Mark Pawlak.

Library of Congress Cataloging-in-Publication Data available on request.
    ISBN 1-931236-63-1 (paperback)
    ISBN 1-931236-62-3 (cloth)

Produced at The Print Center, Inc. 225 Varick St., New York, NY 10014, a non-profit facility for literary and arts-related publications. (212) 206-8465

Table of Contents

In Memory of Dick Humphreys

Author's Note

A few years ago when I started writing these autobiographical sketches, I thought of them as individual pieces. One day I would write about a bullying teacher in the third grade, the next time it might be how I crossed paths with Michael Rockefeller when I was a company clerk in the army. My purpose in each piece was to learn something about myself, with the goal of understanding my own life—something which now seems a bit grandiose and which, of course, I didn't succeed in doing.

I've done my best to remember things honestly, though I make no claims that what I've written is *the* truth. In some cases I've changed the names of individuals; however, I've kept my father's and my brother's names. They were so important and overwhelming to me when I was younger that I'm not comfortable referring to them in a different way than I have all my life.

Somewhere along the way I started putting the pieces in order, "shuffling them around," as Dick Humphreys, my old writing mentor used to advise doing. He believed that from such shuffling of pieces the unconscious would create a satisfactory narrative. I hope it has.

My Mother and Father

My mother pulled me out of kindergarten after a few weeks because I didn't like it, she said. I don't remember it that way. I recall looking out my bedroom window, which faced the schoolyard, shouting at children during recess and wanting to join them. My mother was lonely. My brother Mort, who was almost four years older, was becoming more independent, home for just a minute or two for a glass of milk after school before meeting his friends. My sister Estelle had died the year before I was born, and I was her replacement. When I was five I found her skates in the closet as well as birthday cards from her seventh birthday, her last. It was something my parents didn't discuss with me, though Mort had a few hazy memories of her. I was convinced I would die at seven also, that everyone, in fact, did, and that my parents had managed to disguise this unpleasant fact—universal death at seven.

So I was easily suggestible when it came to illness. If I coughed my mother was ready to put me to bed and I was willing to go. I was thin and fragile looking, though I'm sure I was healthy enough. But I spent a lot of time in bed like an invalid, drinking orange juice squeezed by my mother and inhaling fumes from the vaporizer so I wouldn't develop pneumonia. My mother's two brothers had died of diphtheria in Europe when they were teenagers, and every day my mother squeezed a large glass of blood for me from steak obtained on the black market, since meat was rationed during the war.

My father worked late every day and didn't say much at home. He had mostly been on his own since he was around ten, attending yeshivas in Poland and Germany in order to get an education, and he wasn't sympathetic to weakness or the kind of fragility and nervousness my mother suffered from. Later in life I could never explain to him the potential helpfulness of psychotherapy, which he felt was all a lot of unnecessary talk.

I was known as my mother's child and my brother was my father's. My brother did indeed seem blessed with a sunny, regular disposition and a sturdy, indestructible body. In many ways he became like a parent to me because my mother and father felt at a loss as to how to bring up children in a new country. When I was healthy I trailed after my brother, and he became the disciplinarian. He made me eat vegetables so I would become strong and a good athlete. He taught me to put out my arm for two punches from him or his friends when the mood hit him. And when I didn't practice the piano he threw out my copy of *Lucky To Be A Yankee* by Joe DiMaggio.

I wonder if things would have been different if I'd been the older brother and had the power over him. It's impossible to tell because, as we got older, I was the one who was expected to keep my mother company at dinner. She grew increasingly strange, talking to herself as she crocheted in the living room all day. Her social skills atrophied from disuse. If I ate out she warned me I might be poisoned by germs, and I half-believed her, afraid of dying as I was. My father often boasted how much I loved my mother, but I felt imprisoned.

When we moved downtown from Washington Heights my mother became even more isolated. The only time she went out was to shop for food. Occasionally I went with her and was appalled to see how the tradesmen resented her. She always wanted the freshest and the best and suspected that the storekeepers were passing off inferior fruit or meat on her. When she left she'd slip a dollar to the clerks, but they never looked appeased. Shopping wore my mother out, and she'd go home and take a few sleeping pills.

My father took her retreat personally, as if she were fading away in order to irritate him. She could no longer go out to business dinners or nightclubs, and she made it almost impossible to have friends to the house. In some ways this should have suited my father because he had many girlfriends and this gave him the freedom to go out as he pleased. But he wanted my mother to obey him and do what he saw as her duty as a faithful wife. My father was an intelligent, successful man, often humane and sympathetic at work, someone people came to for advice with their problems, but he lacked any insight into his relationship with my mother. She'd been there with him at his humble beginnings and witnessed his triumphs in business and society, but then she'd broken down like an old horse. While he wasn't ready to send her to the glue factory, he could barely be in the same room without saying something angry or sarcastic. My mother had a pleasant voice and liked to sing popular songs from the Twenties and Thirties, but whenever she did, he would say something like, "Don't finish it, Dearie," and she'd stop, like a canary whose cage had been covered. Clearly he was the stronger of the two and had bested her over the years, but it gave him no pleasure. In fact, her weakness only seemed to make him more incensed.

She died at eighty-seven. Six years before, she had swallowed thirty or so sleeping pills, but survived. "I couldn't even succeed at killing myself," she said to me half-jokingly. In her last years she seemed resigned to waiting for a death from natural causes. When she died my father was sorrowful, even remorseful, for a few days, but then he resumed his life, which in many ways was now easier. He went out with his friends and kept going to his office, and thrived at being a vigorous elder statesman. He still saw women now and then, but never really grew close to anyone in particular. Before, he'd had his wife as his cover; now it was his age. Intimacy with a woman was not something he craved. He did seem to mellow as he grew older, and was more affectionate and attentive to me. But when he spoke about my mother he remained angry. I tried to defend her, telling him she'd had a hard life and that she'd done the best she could, but he never was convinced. He'd given her everything, he said. What more could she have asked for?

Part I   Just a Kid

Just a Kid

I was just a kid. Everything was the way it was supposed to be. I just wanted to fit in. That was my job. Go to the movies on Saturday afternoon, get a frozen custard afterward, play ball in the schoolyard, do my reports in school, color in maps of the Caribbean.

I remember the Chinese laundry and the drugstore at 187th Street and Fort Washington Avenue when I was growing up and Kurtzman's Candy Store at the top of the stairs on the opposite corner. Everything seemed so permanent then.

Who knew RiteAid would knock all the small stores out of business? Somewhere there are men with vision who see ahead and predict trends, like Alvin Toffler, whose *Future Shock* we all read in the Sixties. But I was like the druggist at the corner with his lunch counter and soda fountain, thinking this was the way things would always be.

Older Brother

Saturday afternoon. My brother and his friend Bernie are taking me to the movies. My father is working as usual and my mother is at a luncheon for a local charity. She has made us tuna fish sandwiches and, as a special reward to my brother for taking care of me, she has set out three large slices of strawberry shortcake on her special china.

At seven I am a slow, picky eater and I nibble at my sandwich. My brother and Bernie are supposed to meet friends at the corner on the way to the RKO Coliseum at 181st Street and Broadway. We're late and the two of them gulp down their cake and put on their jackets.

I am still working on my sandwich.

"You'll have to eat yours on the way," my brother says, wrapping my cake in a napkin. We take the elevator down and he and Bernie step quickly into the lobby and head toward the front door of the apartment building. My cake is oozing through the napkin and I stop to take a bite. I like being the only one left with cake. It's as if my brother and Bernie never had any. Often at dinner I savor my dessert the same way to annoy my brother.

"C'mon, we're in a hurry," he shouts.

But I want to finish the cake before it drips to the ground and I take another bite.

"Damn it," my brother says. "Why do I always have to get stuck with you?"

I take another bite and slowly lick the goo off my lips.

"That's it, " my brother says. He rushes toward me and smashes the cake into my face.

I let out a loud scream and start howling, tears rolling down the cake, which is smeared on my cheeks.

"We're going," my brother says. "I've had enough of you."

He and Bernie rush out to the street. I continue crying for several minutes. Then I go back upstairs and take out my key and open the door to the apartment. I put the soggy napkin in the sink and sit down at the kitchen table and wait for my mother to return so I can tell her what my brother did.

First Theft

During the Second World War penny bubblegum was scarce. The only place my friends and I could find it was at Stein's Candy Store at the top of the hill on 187th Street, near Cabrini Boulevard. Mr. Stein made us buy a candy bar for a nickel with every piece of bubblegum he sold us. He was old and mean and we hated him. The candy bars in his store were stale and not the brands we liked. We preferred to go down the hill to Kurtzman's, where they were friendly, but for some reason Mr. Kurtzman wasn't able to procure bubblegum.

One day four of my friends and I each bought a piece of bubblegum and the obligatory candy bar at Stein's. When Mr. Stein turned around to the cash register, each of us, without having planned it, grabbed another candy bar. We threw the candy bars in a trashcan at the bottom of the hill and started laughing hysterically. The gum tasted especially good and we felt pleased with ourselves.

Pet Turtle

I returned our kitten to the grocery store a week after we'd gotten it because it had jumped up on my father and scratched his shoes. My mother offered me a turtle as a replacement. I wanted fish, but my mother was a fastidious housekeeper and said a fish tank would be too much for her to take care of. My mother and I went to a nearby pet store and bought a small terrarium and a turtle with a brightly painted red shell, which I found out later was not healthy for it.

My new turtle moved around the terrarium constantly, swimming back and forth and exploring the little rock above the water. It ate all the food I kept shaking in.

I believed it knew me and came to me when I called. I put it in my hand and let it crawl around. I was a little queasy at its dampness, but also pleased at our intimacy. I cleaned the tank and changed the water regularly. Even my brother, who said turtles were for kids, praised my devotion and diligence. Once, when I tapped my fingernail against the tank, the turtle darted away through the water. That amused me and I began clicking my finger against the glass frequently. When I did this the turtle pulled its head in. I knew this was a cruel thing to do, but I couldn't resist the feeling of power it gave me.

Within a week the turtle grew listless, rarely swimming around and crawling the way it once had done. One day I found it floating lifelessly in the tank and I began bawling. My mother felt so bad for me that she took me to the lot across the street where we buried the turtle and marked its grave with a Popsicle stick. That evening I continued to cry. My parents thought it was sweet that I was so heartbroken over a turtle. They didn't know I was suffering the guilty conscience of a murderer.

A Lack of Love

In the third grade we had to stand by our desks every morning while a monitor inspected our hands and our clothing. Then our teacher Miss Costello would ask what we'd eaten for breakfast. Gayle Bryden always had the best meal—hot cereal, scrambled eggs, toast, bacon, orange juice, and milk. That's the way to start the day, Miss Costello would say, dismissing what the rest of us had eaten. Gayle dressed neatly and had brunette pigtails. She was well behaved and, though she was somewhat aloof, she was well liked and admired. The rest of us envied her big breakfast, not so much because we went hungry but because we also wanted to be praised by Miss Costello, whose enthusiasm for what Gayle had eaten seemed to imply a lack of love and care on the part of our own mothers.

All to Yourself

Arnold Rosen and I used to stand on the low green metal railing in front of the hedge around his apartment building and peek through the bathroom window at his sister in the bathtub. She was in the eighth grade and had large breasts. After looking at her we'd walk around the neighborhood, imagining what it was like to be a girl and have asts all to yourself.

Musical Prodigy

When I was little I used to sing for company. My parents and their friends would sit in the living room while I shyly positioned myself out of sight in the foyer and serenaded them with "Don't Fence Me In" or "Mairzy Doats." Everyone would applaud wildly at the end and tell me I was a musical prodigy. My parents thought I would be a natural at the piano, so when I was nine they purchased a small upright one, but when it was delivered it didn't fit into the elevator. Our building, 660 Fort Washington Avenue, didn't have a freight elevator and we lived on the fifth floor.

I came home for lunch one June day and discovered that several burly movers had taken out the windows from the bedroom my brother and I shared, and were dangling ropes down to several co-workers who were standing on the sidewalk next to the piano. Our bedroom looked out on the schoolyard, which was beginning to fill with children. Most of them were standing by the fence, looking at the spectacle. But after the workers wrapped the piano in canvas and tied it with rope and began to pull it up, the sky suddenly grew black and a heavy summer rain fell. I could hear the surprised, excited gasps of the children as they raced to the school's entrance to escape the downpour. The movers strained as they hoisted the piano up and cursed the rain that swept into the room. Finally they managed to angle the piano inside and shove it against the wall facing our beds.

The rain soon stopped and the sun came out and I rushed back to school, eager to revel in everyone's attention. Sure enough, my classmates kept chattering about the piano. Even Miss Costello couldn't silence them. It was one of the big events of the year.

At three o'clock I rushed home and sat on the stool and started to play, but was disappointed that I could produce only clunky, disconnected sounds. I had been convinced I was such a prodigy that I would be able to play songs immediately.

In the fall I began taking lessons from Mrs. Parker, a plump, cheerful woman who soon had me playing simple songs, like "Early One Morning." In December she held a concert for her students and I tied for first place. My prize was a large book with a bright red cover, *Stories of the Great Operas*, which Mrs. Parker inscribed to me and which my mother placed prominently on the coffee table in front of the sofa.

Unfortunately for me, the reason for Mrs. Parker's plumpness was that she was pregnant, and a month or two later she gave birth and could no longer travel to our house to give me lessons. Mr. Fishman, who lived nearby, replaced her. He dressed in a suit and tie and spoke with a German accent. He began by teaching me musical theory and assigned me written homework, along with simplified versions of Beethoven pieces to practice. He was strict and short-tempered and I sat sullenly through his lessons and soon stopped practicing. My parents tried to encourage me, telling me how sorry I'd be when I got older. But I'd look out the window during lessons and wish I was playing baseball in the schoolyard with my friends. One day, as my team was about to begin an important game and Mr. Fishman was demonstrating for the third time how to play "The Turkish Rondo," my tears began to fall onto the piano keys.

"What's wrong?" Mr. Fishman asked. When I told him, he sighed and instructed me to go downstairs and join the game. That was my last piano lesson.

One Monday Morning

One Monday morning after a heavy snowfall Arnold Rosen scooped up grains of rock salt that had been scattered on the sidewalk near the entrance to the schoolyard at P.S. 187 and put them in his pocket. When we got to our classroom he casually walked toward his seat at the front of the room and dumped the salt in the big open bottle of dark blue ink on Miss Costello's desk. Every Monday morning Miss Costello would place a paper cone over the top of the bottle and fill the inkwells on our desks so that we could dip our pens and copy down what she wrote on the blackboard. But with the addition of the rock salt our pens wouldn't write, no matter how hard we pressed.

Miss Costello stirred the bottle with a ruler. "Someone has sabotaged the ink," she said, her face becoming as bright as her dyed red hair. "That person better confess or I'll keep the whole class in after school."

Arnold and I lived in neighboring apartment buildings and played together after school every day. My brother was the one who had told him about the effects of rock salt on ink.

Everyone kept looking around the room, trying to guess who the culprit was. I felt guilty because I knew and I was worried Miss Costello would be able to tell. I wished Arnold would own up to what he'd done. It didn't seem fair that everyone had to stay after school. When the dismissal bell rang at three, Miss Costello stood in front of the room and asked us one at a time if we knew anything about the ink. Arnold shook his head, his eyes big and innocent looking. I shook my head also, but Miss Costello stared at me in a way that made me feel she suspected me. Time passed very slowly. We could hear the shouts of children as they threw snowballs at one another in the schoolyard. Finally, at four, Miss Costello made us stand beside our seats. "The person who did this will have it on his conscience and I'll be watching," she said. Arnold and I walked home together but we didn't talk and fool around as we usually did. When I reached my building's entrance I turned in without saying goodbye. After that we stopped playing together.

Best Friend

Herbie Bernstein's one fault was that he couldn't stop talking and sometimes said things that were taken the wrong way by other boys. But he was very entertaining and I hoped he would become my best friend. One day in the schoolyard Herbie started teasing Joel Leibowitz. Joel was a large, powerful boy who looked much older than he was. He had intelligent eyes and wasn't known as a bully, but all of a sudden Joel and Herbie were circling one another and everyone in the schoolyard was watching. Herbie, who was slender and short, kept saying he wasn't afraid of a moron like Joel. Without thinking, I moved in front of him and, to my own surprise, spat at Joel, who shifted out of the way, but a little of my saliva landed on his shoulder. Now his irritation switched to me, which must have been what I wanted to happen, but it all occurred so fast that I'm not sure I actually knew what I was doing.

Joel and I faced each other with raised fists. He seemed immense, his hands and arms twice as big as mine. Herbie, right behind me, called Joel a big creampuff. I wanted him to keep quiet, but I was too nervous to say anything. Joel feinted a punch at my head and I raised my hands to block him and he lowered his right hand and shot a fist to my stomach, right below my solar plexus. His punch hurt but not as badly as I expected. I was relieved. I had been afraid of getting seriously hurt or even killed. I fell to the ground and let out a loud, exaggerated groan and stayed motionless for a minute or so. Then I staggered up. Joel and I shook hands and the crowd moved away, somewhat disappointed. Soon Herbie and I started walking home. "He hit you with a lucky punch," Herbie said. "Otherwise you would have destroyed him." I felt like telling him to shut up, but I said nothing, not wanting to hurt my new best friend's feelings.

Looking For Money

All my friends and I wanted to do in the whole world was to continue playing stepball on the flight of stairs leading up to the schoolyard, but we didn't have the fifty cents to buy a new Spaldeen. Our old one had just split beyond repair and we had only a few pennies, but we felt too old to go home and ask our mothers for money, so we stood around brainstorming until one of us suggested that we search for money in the streets. This sounded like a good idea and we started walking up Fort Washington Avenue, two of us on the curb side, the other two alongside the hedges in front of the apartment houses. Almost immediately Herbie found a nickel near the curb. Then Larry spotted a quarter in the dirt in the hedges. We continued walking north toward Fort Tryon Park, certain there was more gold in the streets and, sure enough, before we came to the last apartment house we found two dimes and a nickel. We rushed to Kurtzman's and bought a ball and, with the extra nickel, a candy bar that we shared.

Later in life I found five dollars several times and once a twenty dollar bill, but nothing was as sweet as the fifty-five cents we found that day on Fort Washington Avenue. Sometimes I wonder if this memory is really a dream, and I wish I still knew Larry and Herbie and Artie so I could ask them if they remember how we looked for money that day.

Falling Behind

One year my family spent the winter in Florida and I attended the Mannheim School, a private school where the children sat around tables under brightly colored umbrellas and chatted with one another all day, with no direction from the teachers. In the spring when I returned to New York, my teacher Miss McCloskey sent me to the front of the classroom and asked me questions about social studies. What was Chicago famous for? she asked. I didn't know and Miss McCloskey called on another student, who said Chicago was the meat center of America. She asked me several other questions, which I couldn't answer either. Finally, with a withering look, she sent me back to my seat. "It's not his fault," she said to the class. "I just wanted everyone to know that you can't miss three months in the fourth grade without falling behind."

My Mother and Miss Roberts

After Miss Burke, my fifth grade teacher, wrote a note home complaining about my frequent talking in class and asking my parents to come see her, my mother devised her own plan of defense. She would go to see Miss Roberts, the principal, instead. My mother was sure Miss Roberts would be more understanding of the mischievous energy of a healthy, normal young boy than Miss Burke, who had a reputation for being mean and tough.

My mother planned her strategy carefully. She would dress in her finest—a black felt hat with a small veil, an expensive dress, open-toed, high-heeled shoes, and her mink coat. For visits to the dentist or doctor my mother dressed down, not wanting to appear rich and be charged a high rate, but on this occasion she wanted to impress Miss Roberts with our family's wealth and importance.

My mother had visited Miss Roberts before, when we had gone to Florida for the winter and my brother and I missed several months of school. My mother brought an expensive bottle of French perfume on our return, which Miss Roberts accepted, assuring my mother that two smart boys like her sons could make up for the work they missed in no time. After that my mother was proud of her friendship with Miss Roberts and referred to it often.

A few days after receiving the note my mother told me she was going to see her old friend Miss Roberts later that morning and would straighten everything out. I wasn't too happy about her plans, but I said nothing. When she was older my mother had a limited repertoire of stories that she constantly repeated, and the visit to Miss Roberts was one of them.

My mother arrived at the appointed time and was ushered into Miss Roberts' office, where the two of them drank tea and talked casually like old friends. Miss Roberts was a sturdy woman with a steadfast gaze and blonde hair, which was reputed by some students to be a wig. She had a slight lisp that we imitated in the schoolyard each week after she addressed us at assembly in the auditorium. Midway in the visit my mother presented Miss Roberts with another bottle of perfume, a gesture of appreciation, she said, for the wonderful job she was doing for all the children in the neighborhood. Then my mother mentioned the note from Miss Burke, and Miss Roberts said she thought it would be a good idea to go to the classroom and find out how things were going. She and my mother walked slowly down the hall, chatting away. When they reached the classroom, Miss Roberts ushered my mother in and the students stared at them. My mother looked beautiful and impressive in her hat and coat, like a visiting dignitary. "Good morning, Miss Roberts," Miss Burke said in a soft, respectful way, unlike the tone she ordinarily used with us. All the other kids were staring at the two visitors.

"I was just talking with Mrs. Schrader," Miss Roberts said, "and I wondered how her son is doing."

"Why he's doing just fine. He's one of our best boys."

"I'm pleased to hear that," Miss Roberts said, and she thanked Miss Burke and left with my mother.

Miss Burke was quieter than usual the rest of the morning, and I was too. I was embarrassed by my mother's appearance in class with the principal. The rest of the year I was a model student, not wanting my mother to return to school.

Roosevelt

Word that Franklin Roosevelt had died spread through the school during the day. At three o'clock we milled outside in the schoolyard talking about it. It was a warm spring day, but it felt like the end of the world. How could we win the war without our leader? I hated the Germans, not because they were killing my relatives—my family had told me nothing about that—but because they were our enemies and spoke with funny accents in war movies. At night I dreamed I was able to single-handedly defeat the German army. I collected empty cigarette packs from friends of my parents and rolled the silver foil into a big ball and brought it to school for the war effort.

The only ones who were critical of the war and didn't like Roosevelt were my classmate Richard McGonigle and his older brother, Patrick. They read a lot and weren't good athletes and they didn't have many friends. They lived with their mother, who rarely spoke to anyone.

"It serves him right," Patrick said that afternoon in the schoolyard. "He never should have brought us into the war." Billy Newman, who lived below me and was the best basketball player in school, ran toward Patrick and punched him in the face. They rolled onto the ground, with Billy on top. When Patrick got up, his nose was bleeding and he was sobbing. We all jeered at him and pushed him as he squeezed past us toward the gate.

Soon his mother rushed into the schoolyard and started shouting at us. "You're a bunch of cowards! You've no right to beat my son up! I'll get the police after you!" She stormed up the stairs into the school to complain.

As far as I know, Billy didn't get into trouble and that was the last we heard about it. No one spoke to either of the McGonigle brothers for the rest of the term. By September when school began again, they had moved from the neighborhood.

Xavier Cugat

Weekend nights my brother and his friends used to hang out at the corner candy store near the top of the stairs at Fort Washington Avenue and 187th Street. They wore leather jackets and smoked cigars, or at least pretended to, as they flirted with girls and made smart remarks. My brother boasted to me that he'd seen Xavier Cugat, the band leader, at the candy store many times. Cugat was courting Frances Lassman, later known as Abby Lane, who was in my brother's eighth grade class at P.S. 187. She was beautiful and wasn't allowed to go out with any of the boys in the neighborhood. According to my brother she was destined for more important things in life—a musical career and marriage to someone successful. Xavier Cugat was then in his thirties, at the height of his fame, and we all knew him from the movies and from photos in newspapers in which he stood in front of his orchestra, his Chihuahua cradled in one hand as he conducted with the other. Or else he'd be alone in the picture, smiling, his pencil-thin mustache curling upwards as he puffed a cigar. Cugat often stopped at the corner to buy himself a cigar. He'd pull up in his black Cadillac, walk briskly into the candy store, and nod to the boys on his way out. Then he'd drive up the hill to Cabrini Boulevard to the six-story apartment house where his future wife Frances lived.

Portrait

My first brush with the artistic life came when my mother took me to have my portrait painted by Arnold Hoffman, who, according to her, was a widely known artist. My brother refused to go. He had just discovered girls and told my mother he was too busy. My mother said he'd be sorry when he grew older and realized what an opportunity he had missed, and she praised my maturity for being willing to sit. I really didn't want to go either, but it was established in our family that my job was to keep my mother happy.

I was, to judge from the photos of me at the time, a handsome little boy. In fact I think I peaked at nine or ten. I had reddish brown hair and rosy cheeks and dimples. People used to ask if I slept on collar buttons and would pinch my cheeks. With my coloring, I was considered gentile-looking, which pleased my family since we were trying to be American. My father was doing well in business and my mother considered us to be socially above most of the other families in Washington Heights. My mother was artistic and had been an art student when she first came to the United States from Warsaw. When she was a young child she had attended the opera and museums, and she looked down her nose at neighbors, particularly Mrs. Goodman with her bad taste, who lived above us and claimed that one of the chairs in her living room once belonged to Louis XIV.

My mother liked to go to Third Avenue to the stores under the El where she searched for authentic antiques at bargain prices. Now we would be the only family in the neighborhood to have art painted by a famous artist. Hoffman had a studio near Klein's at 14th Street to which my mother and I rode the A train downtown from the Heights. I wasn't happy at first, since I missed playing with my friends after school. But my mother let me stand in the front car of the train and look out the windows at the changing lights along the tracks and I soon forgot about my friends.

Hoffman dressed the part of an artist—corduroy pants, a black turtleneck and a tweed jacket. He was cheerful and friendly. He told me I was a wonderful subject. At first I had trouble holding a pose very long, and he placed his enormous grey cat on my lap for me to play with. The cat was old and fat and lay sleepily against me as I rubbed my hands on her belly. As long as I petted her she purred contentedly. I particularly enjoyed holding her since we were not allowed to have pets at home. They were too messy, and my father didn't want them tearing at his clothing and shoes. So I sat quietly and looked around at the studio with its high ceilings and large windows and inhaled the strong, delicious smell of paint. I usually sank into a sort of trance, petting the cat and feeling the vibrations of its purring against my body.

My mother sat quietly also, enjoying the artist's concentration and quick movements. She always dressed in a simple cloth coat for our visits, the way she did whenever we went anywhere that she had to pay for a service. She was afraid that Hoffman would think she was wealthy and double his price.

Once I combed my hair differently than I had the previous day and Hoffman scolded me. I offered to comb it back the way it had been but he told me to remain still so he could retouch my hair in the portrait.

After the last session my mother paid Hoffman the final installment and told him the painting was a masterpiece. He wrapped brown paper around the canvas and we took a cab home so the painting wouldn't be damaged in the subway. That evening my mother showed it to my brother and father. My brother wasn't too impressed, but my father admired it for a long time. Hoffman had painted an idealized version of me, making me look several years older, in a sport jacket and open shirt, staring out like a young English nobleman. "It could be in a museum," my father said.

A few years later we moved downtown to Central Park West and my mother hung the portrait above the non-working fireplace in the living room. Whenever my friends came over I made disparaging remarks about the painting, but secretly I was pleased that my likeness was on the wall. I felt it showed my importance within the family. The painting hung there for fifty years until both of my parents died and my brother and I sold the apartment. Naturally, I got to keep the portrait, but it didn't go with the rest of the things in our place. My wife and I put it in a storage room in the basement with the other odds and ends that we have accumulated over the years and have little use for, but don't have the heart to throw out.

Comedian

At P.S. 187 Christmas parties I performed as a comedian and fantasized having my own radio show. Most of my material was about the Second World War. I did imitations of Hitler and Hirohito. My highlight was Mussolini pleading for his life right before he was stomped to death. "Pleasa don'ta kill me!" I shouted. "Pleasa don't step on my head!"

Everything went great until the sixth grade when, during my Mussolini routine, I noticed Susan Seidman, the prettier of the Seidman twins, looking at me in a bored, critical way, as if she didn't believe how stupid and näive I could be. She and her sister Marian were the epitome of female refinement and beauty. Susan played the piano and Marian the violin in the school orchestra. They were model students and had a small circle of friends who were similarly cultivated. I was a member of the Royals, a group of boys who played baseball or basketball in the afternoon and hung out on the corner at night.

While I was still doing Mussolini, Miss Brenner, the teacher, twisted her mouth to one side, the way she did when she was annoyed, and asked if I would be finished soon. I had more material prepared, including a radio advertisement for Mrs. Murphy's matzo balls, which bounced on the floor and could be used as baseballs, but I ended my routine abruptly and sat down. Times had changed. My material was flat—the war was over, and so was my career as a comedian.

Stretching Paul Lansky

After my brother was beaten up in the schoolyard by an older boy, my father decided to send him to George Brown's gym on West 57th Street. As an afterthought he sent me too. I was eleven, chubby, a good athlete, still reasonably happy.

The gym was on the top floor of an office building between 6th and 7th Avenues. It had weights, a few exercise machines, a four-wall handball court, and a boxing ring. George had been a ranked fighter in his time and had supposedly been in the ring with Jack Dempsey. He had an assistant, Jimmy, a handsome Irishman with graying hair and a slight brogue, who had once been a good club fighter.

I was the youngest person at the gym and everyone paid special attention to me. George knew many celebrities and prominent people, and members included one of the Gimbels from the department store family, and Quentin Reynolds, the well-known columnist and author, and, most famous of all, Ernest Hemingway. I never saw Hemingway there but he and George were good friends and they boxed together when Hemingway visited New York from Havana.

Often I played racquetball with Quentin Reynolds, who was middle-aged and had a pot belly. He'd stand in the center of the court and smack the little black ball and make it carom off the walls. "Good hustle, kid," he'd say after I'd try unsuccessfully to run the ball down. "You'll be good one day. Get to know all the angles." I believed him, but I could never win more than a few points, no matter how hard I tried.

My brother, wearing a big protective helmet and padded gloves, would hit the punching bag and spar with Jimmy. Jimmy would dart in and out, shouting instructions. Punch, he'd say as he slipped inside my brother's jabs or slapped them away. He'd glide around the ring as if he were weightless, able to anticipate my brother's moves. Jimmy wanted to enter my brother in the Golden Gloves tournament, but my father wouldn't let him because he was afraid my brother would get hurt.

I worked out with Jimmy, too, throwing big wild punches that he chuckled at. He said I had potential, and I'd be better than my brother when I got bigger. I looked forward to going to the gym a couple of times a week, working out with Jimmy, playing racquetball with Quentin Reynolds, and fooling around on the exercise machines.

One of the other members we got to know was Paul, a short, thin young man a couple of years older than my brother. His father was Meyer Lansky, the Jewish gangster. Paul sparred with Jimmy every day and sometimes with my brother, though Jimmy made sure that the two of them didn't hurt each other. Paul was quiet and soft-spoken and he and my brother became friends.

After he worked out Paul would lie down on a training table and Jimmy and George would stand at opposite ends and pull him, Jimmy by the head and George by the feet. They'd let out little grunts as they tugged him, while Paul would lie there silently with his eyes closed.

My brother explained to me that Paul wanted to go to the West Point Military Academy, but was an inch too short, and George and Jimmy were stretching him to make him bigger. If I was nearby I'd stop and watch.

After about six months Paul reached the required height of five foot six, and was admitted to West Point. We all congratulated him, but when it became public that Meyer Lansky's son was going there, criticism hit the newspapers. Quentin Reynolds defended Paul's admission in one of his newspaper columns, saying that in a democracy anybody should be able to go to West Point, *even* a gangster's son. Paul attended in the fall and eventually became the welterweight champion there.

A couple of years ago I came across a biography of Meyer Lansky in a bookstore and looked up Paul. I learned that he served eight years in the Army Air Force, attaining the rank of captain, before going to work for the Apollo space program. I pictured him living in a suburb in Arizona, standing in the back yard of his house, cleaning the grill after dinner, looking up at the evening sky, and remembering George and Jimmy pulling him from different ends to make him bigger.

Television

The year we got our TV was 1947, when I was eleven. We were one of the first families on the block to buy one, and since my older brother and I were the ones who had pleaded for it, we placed the TV set on the desk in our bedroom. The set, which I think was an Emerson, had a small screen with black and white reception, since color didn't exist yet. When we first got the TV, I would sometimes tell my mother I was sick when I got up in the morning so that I could stay home from school and watch it. My mother didn't mind. In fact, she liked squeezing orange juice and bringing cups of tea to me all day. I would watch Channel 13, which at the time was a small station in Newark, New Jersey, that repeated the same feature movie all day. If I liked the movie, I'd watch it over and over.

The shows I enjoyed the most were the variety ones at night, particularly Milton Berle and Ed Sullivan. The Ed Sullivan show always opened with a chorus line of beautiful dancers in scanty outfits, who moved gracefully and kicked their legs in unison. These programs introduced me to a sophistication and humor that didn't exist at home, where we ate meals in silence and then afterwards my father would sit in his armchair in the living room and study the day's stock market results in the evening paper.

One Sunday night my brother and I and our Uncle Jack, who was married to my father's sister Laura, were sitting on my brother's bed waiting for the Ed Sullivan show to begin. Laura was several years older than Jack and had married at thirty, late for a woman then. Jack was dreamy and good natured, and was the only relative in the family who took the effort to talk and play with my brother and me. But he was never able to make much money and, at Laura's insistence, had tried and failed at several business ventures. One was a laundry service that made pickups at customers' apartments and delivered the clean clothing a few days later. But Jack wasn't organized, and clothing was often delivered to the wrong customer, so he had to close. He took me with him one day when I was small and we drove all over the city in his small truck. He let me hold the wheel while we were moving. Driving wasn't that common in the city then. Washington Heights didn't even have parking regulations or traffic lights.

That night, just as the women in the chorus line of the Ed Sullivan show danced onto the screen on their long, shapely legs, Laura, who'd been in the living room with my parents, burst into the bedroom. "How dare you look at those women!" Laura screamed at Jack. "I won't have it!" Jack stood up obediently and left the room with her. For a moment I felt sorry for him, since he had to miss all the fun, but then I forgot about him as I turned back to watch the show. I didn't question Laura's bossiness or meanness. That was how adults were. They had their own lives and rules, and I didn't care what they did as long as I could watch as much television as I wanted to.

Part II The Ways of the World

First Cigarette

When I was twelve I spent the summer with my parents at the Oceancrest Hotel in Long Beach, Long Island. I had been going to summer camp in Pennsylvania since I was seven, but the previous winter I mentioned to my mother that my counselor, Big Steve, had kicked me in the ass while wearing his army boots. My mother was horrified, and she and my father immediately decided not to send my brother and me back. They found another camp for my brother on Schroon Lake near Ticonderoga, New York, but because I was younger and more delicate, they decided to keep me with them. So I was stuck at the Oceancrest with my parents and my Uncle Ben and Ben's wife Rita, a lively blonde with a voluptuous figure, and the other guests, most of them elderly.

My father was away all day at work. Occasionally I played Ping-Pong with the porters in the basement. They were friendly, decent men who slept in one big damp dorm room near the Ping-Pong table. My parents discouraged me from spending time with them. They never said exactly why, but it was clear they didn't feel it was socially advantageous for me to be friendly with older, poorly educated black men.

The days were passable because I hung out at the beach and swam in the ocean. In the evening I was supposed to stay in front of the hotel and sit with my parents and their friends on rockers that the porters brought out to the boardwalk for quarter tips. The adults talked in a mixture of English and Yiddish that I disliked because it sounded so old-fashioned.

I took walks on the boardwalk and discovered a skee-ball concession.

I learned to roll the wooden balls down the short lane into small round holes. The farthest one was worth fifty points. I soon was able to spin the ball off the side of the lane consistently into the fifty hole and win many coupons. Above the skee-ball lanes were prizes—toasters, portable radios, fans, and large dolls. I kept my coupons in a large shoe box that was rapidly filling.

Each night my father gave me a few dollars and sometimes my Uncle Ben threw in some more, and for an hour or so I would manage to escape my boredom and loneliness as I played skee-ball. As I got better, people sometimes gathered in admiration to watch me. But my money would only last so long, and then, with twenty cents that I always put away at the beginning, I bought a large custard cone and walked another quarter of a mile or so to the end of the boardwalk, then back to the hotel where people would still be sitting in rockers. Occasionally I snuck down to the basement to see if any of the porters was available to play Ping-Pong.

My mother sat on the beach all day and crocheted and kept watch as I swam, even though there was a lifeguard. My mother had lots of rules—I had to wait an hour after breakfast and after lunch before going in the water so I wouldn't get stomach cramps; and I had to wear a hat to prevent sunstroke. Occasionally someone my age passed through the hotel. One night in the lobby I met a twelve-year-old girl who spoke with an English accent. She seemed as bored as I was, and late in the evening we held hands and kissed goodnight in a deserted part of the lobby, but she was gone the next day.

One night in late August I bought a pack of cigarettes at a store on the boardwalk. I told the man they were for my father. I wanted to look older and sophisticated and pick up a girl. After I played skee-ball I walked toward the end of the boardwalk and opened the pack and lit a cigarette, which made me cough, but I kept puffing to keep it lit. I felt debonair as I held the cigarette to my mouth and then brought it to my side with a flourish, keeping on the lookout for a lone girl. I walked slowly, glancing sideways, and suddenly came face to face with my father and Uncle Ben. It was too late for me to discard the cigarette so I nodded to them and kept walking. My father looked at me with a bemused expression. Uncle Ben, an outgoing man who spent his afternoons at the track, smiled. As soon as they were out of sight I stubbed the cigarette out. When I got back to the hotel I gave the pack to one of the porters.

My father never said anything to me. I almost wanted him to reprimand me, to tell me I was too young to smoke, but my father never disciplined my brother or me. He left that to my mother.

The next day I went back to the usual routine. Breakfast, an hour's wait until swimming, then lunch and another hour's wait. My mother seemed to have no inkling that my father had seen me smoking, but I was on my best behavior anyway.

Then the summer was over and we went back home. I forget what prize I won at skee-ball, but I think I ended up giving it to one of the porters.

Virginia Gianelli

One of my best friends in the sixth grade was Jerry Mesner, who was thin, red-haired, and talkative. We were the same height, so we entered and left school in line together. I was as used to the slight odor of his breath on the staircase as I was to his red hair. One Friday night when his parents were going out till late, Jerry arranged to bring Virginia Gianelli to his house and invited me and four others over. Virginia was known as someone who let boys feel her up, though usually one at a time. When she entered the apartment with Jerry and saw the other five of us, she looked frightened. Virginia was a brunette with a perky nose and innocent brown eyes and small, budding breasts. Jerry was older by a few months than the rest of us and it was his house, so he was the spokesman.

"We just want to have a little fun," he told her when she said she wasn't sure if she wanted to stay. Virginia sat primly on the sofa, looking around, trying to get her bearings. She was in a different sixth grade class than I was at P.S. 187 and I had never spoken to her, but things get known about a girl who is promiscuous. She was Italian and lived with her mother in a poorer part of the neighborhood and rarely did her homework. We were Jewish, our fathers were professionals or in small businesses. Larry's father sold insurance, as Larry would ten years later. Jerry's father was an investigator for the IRS, Herbie's an inventor. Artie's father, like mine, was a dress contractor, and Ira's father owned the newsstand at 181st Street and Broadway. When I first found out what Ira's father did, I taunted him in the schoolyard, calling him newsboy until he wrestled me to the ground and made me stop making fun of him. I don't know why I acted that way, I just did. Now we were trying to make out with a girl. Making out meant getting a few feels, and Jerry tried to assure Virginia that nothing bad was going to happen.

"We'll give you a fair chance," he said. "We'll play strip poker. Each time you lose you take something off. Each time you win we'll take something off." There were six of us, so the odds were somewhat in our favor. But just to be safe, Jerry hid another deck of cards in his lap.

As he dealt, Jerry kept calling out the possible combinations for each player, and somehow one of us would always miraculously draw a fourth ace or king on the last card, but Virginia never questioned our luck. She was soon down to her brassiere and panties and then just her panties.

"All right, we won't make you take anything else off," Jerry said. "You go into the bathroom and two of us'll go in at a time, and then you can get dressed."

Virginia agreed. Perhaps she realized that two boys together would behave with more inhibition than if each of us went in singly. Jerry and Herbie were first. Herbie was a dreamy, gentle boy, which was probably why Jerry chose him. He knew Herbie would hold back and Jerry would be able to monopolize the action.

After a couple of minutes they came out. "I felt her pussy hair," Jerry said. "It's scratchy."

Larry and I went next. Virginia was standing in front of the sink, watching us with frightened but curious eyes. Her small breasts rose and fell with her breathing. Her soft, round stomach was enclosed by her panties. Larry reached out and touched her breasts and pinched a nipple. "Ow," Virginia said, "that hurts." I leaned forward and stroked her stomach. Her skin was very white and soft. Our eyes met and she blushed and looked down. I reached up and touched her cheek. I wanted to tell her she was beautiful.

Artie and Ira went in after us and then it was over. Dressed, she looked like any other girl.

I don't remember if Jerry walked her home or if we all left together. Afterwards we graduated to more acceptable ways of getting to know girls and rarely spoke of what we'd done. In school whenever Virginia and I passed in the halls, neither of us acknowledged the other. But I remembered her soft white skin and her blush, and I desired her more than any of the other girls I knew.

The next year I moved downtown and transferred to Franklin, a private school, and soon stopped seeing anyone from the neighborhood. I heard that Herbie didn't go to college and got a job as a groundskeeper for the Parks Department. When I was twenty-two Larry called to sell me life insurance. I don't know about Ira, but a few years ago I saw Jerry's name in the paper as a finalist in a senior tennis tournament. I never heard anything about Virginia.

The Late Pepper

When I was a boy, my experience with pets never turned out well. The kitten I brought home from the grocery store had to be returned, and my turtle with the painted red shell died after a week. Pepper, the beagle I chose at the pet store for my bar mitzvah present, started coughing her first night with us, and by the following afternoon had to be taken to an animal clinic in Inwood, where she was diagnosed with distemper. I visited her there several times, but a week later she died. I learned of Pepper's death at the clinic when the vet looked at me in surprise and asked, "Didn't your parents tell you? We had to put her away last night."

I sat near the window on the subway ride home and tried to hide my tears from the other passengers. I kept crying at dinner, until finally my brother ordered me to stop. "It was just a dog, for Christ's sake. No one cries that much over a dog."

So I stopped crying, not wanting to appear abnormal. A few days later I wrote a composition in school entitled "The Late Pepper," describing how sad I was about my dog. Mr. Hall, our English teacher and the co-owner of the Franklin School, was an old-fashioned gentleman who always wore a three-piece suit, with the vest buttoned and a gold watch chain hanging from it. I received a ninety, by far the highest mark Mr. Hall had ever given me. It would have been even higher if I hadn't misspelled the possessive "its" with an apostrophe before the "s" and hadn't written "everyday" as two words instead of one when I used it as an adjective.

This was the first time I had the sense that I could turn life into art, give suffering meaning, receive recognition, and console myself at the same time. My brother was wrong; grieving for a dog wasn't such a bad thing.

Good Reading

After we moved downtown to an eight-room apartment on Central Park West, I began spending most of my time after school at home because I didn't like the other kids in my class and didn't know anybody else except friends from my old neighborhood in Washington Heights. Once a couple of them came down on a Friday night to play poker in my family's new apartment. They marveled at the huge size of the living room and gasped when I told them the rent was two hundred and ninety-two dollars a month. This neighborhood's too rich for us, they said, and they meant it. If I wanted to see them I had to go uptown, but that was difficult and painful for me now that I was an outsider. I tried playing basketball at the 86th Street courts in Central Park, but there was always a long line, and most of the boys were older and rougher than I was used to.

At home I mostly read. Paperback books were just coming out, and for twenty-five cents or so I had a wide selection. I discovered Brentano's at 48th Street and Fifth Avenue, and around the corner the Gotham Book Mart. I tried *Portrait of the Artist as a Young Man*, but didn't get too far. But I read popular books like George R. Stewart's *Fire* and also *Storm*, and more serious books by writers like Dreiser, Sinclair Lewis, and Upton Sinclair, all of which I found listed in a Mentor paperback entitled *Good Reading*. The editors had organized by century, country, and genre what they thought were the best books ever written. I planned to eventually read everything, but I started by concentrating on 20th century fiction, which was more enjoyable and accessible to me than the classics like Plutarch and Chaucer. About the only time I eased off was on Friday nights, when I watched the fights on television and ate two pints of ice cream.

My mother spent her days crocheting or knitting in the living room, near the window for light, talking to herself and reliving her childhood in Poland. I'd have an early dinner with her and then she'd go to sleep. She was always suffering from some illness and needed rest. My father would come home much later, usually in a good mood after dinner out and a drink or two. If I was up he'd peek in and say hello and shake his head over my constant reading, wondering how he'd gotten a son like me.

Our apartment on Central Park West was palatial, with oak-paneled walls and detailed molding and high ceilings, but it was on the third floor and it was dark most of the day. In Washington Heights we had lived on the fifth floor overlooking the P.S.187 schoolyard. There was a tree outside the window of the bedroom my brother and I shared, and in the spring we watched the leaves bloom. Once a robin made a nest on one of the branches and we saw the eggs hatch. In the winter, when the tree was bare, we could see the Hudson River. Now my bedroom faced the wall of a large apartment building.

Belle, our maid in Washington Heights, had gotten sick and wasn't strong enough to take care of our new large apartment. She was a bright, cheerful woman and I had always enjoyed her company. She gave me snacks in the afternoon after school and told me the score of Yankee games. She ordered my brother and me to pick up our socks and underwear and put them in the hamper. No one should have to do that for another person, she told us. Even my mother, who suspected maids of being lazy and stealing, admitted Belle was different. But now Belle was old and tired and had to be replaced.

The new maid, Ollie, was a light-skinned, formidable-looking woman who wore plain glasses. She was in her mid-fifties and seemed more like a teacher than a maid. I felt intimidated by her serious manner and didn't say much to her. She told my mother she could stay only a year because she had a home in Pennsylvania that she periodically had to take care of.

My mother didn't believe her—a Negro with a house in the country sounded far-fetched to her—but Ollie had good references and my mother needed a maid.

Ollie served meals, washed the dishes, and cleaned the house. My mother did the shopping and cooking, assisted by Ollie. My mother was very particular in the way she prepared food, and didn't trust anybody else to follow her instructions. Belle had been allowed to cook alone, but that was only after a few years with us. My mother conceded that Ollie was intelligent and competent, but she wasn't ready to entrust the kitchen to her.

Ollie slept in a small room along the hallway to the kitchen. The apartment was divided by two long hallways. One was a pantry that led to the kitchen, past Ollie's bedroom and small bathroom. The other hallway, which ran parallel to the pantry, had three bedrooms, two bathrooms and several large closets. So, though Ollie lived with us, I didn't see much of her. I didn't see anyone much, for that matter, except my mother at mealtimes. My father was always working and ate out most nights, and my brother had his own life with his friends outside. When he was home he talked on his private phone in his room. I missed the time when we had shared a bedroom.

One night after reading late I went to the kitchen for a snack and found Ollie at the small breakfast table, drinking a cup of tea. She was in her bathrobe, and I felt that I was intruding on her. I was carrying the book I was reading, *Native Son* by Richard Wright. "You could learn from that book," she said. "I have another one by him." She brought out a paperback, *Uncle Tom's Children*, from her room and handed it to me. "I've finished it," she said, "you can keep it."

Even though I was reading Wright, I had never thought much about Negroes. I knew something about them from *Native Son*, but that was only through reading. I had never wondered about Ollie as a person, for instance, though we had lived in the same apartment for several months. I never thought about Belle either, yet I had known her for years and liked her. Now, even though she was sick and old, I hadn't tried to contact her. She was just someone who once cleaned the house and now she didn't. I was too busy reading novels to think about other people.

"This isn't a happy house," Ollie said. "I've worked in lots of places before."

I felt dizzy as she spoke, as if I were under a microscope.

"Nobody's around much," she went on, "except you and your mother, and you're young and don't have a choice. There's money but not much else."

I wanted to defend my family. We did too love one another, I wanted to say, but deep inside I knew she was right. My father rarely spoke to my mother or me, and my mother mostly spoke to herself. Ollie was right. She had read us like a novel.

"Keep the book," she said. "I've finished it. If you don't read it now, you will someday."

I thanked her and took the book to my bedroom. *Uncle Tom's Children* was a collection of unconnected stories, which I found harder to read than a novel, and I put it aside.

In bed I tried to think about my family. We were like a novel, with our tensions and secrets, except we were an actual family and this was my life. I was unhappy and lonely and didn't know what to do about it.

Ollie never spoke to me about my family again, but I felt defensive in front of her, positive she was observing me in my misery. Yet I also respected her and looked at her differently.

At the end of the year Ollie left to return to Pennsylvania as she had said she would. When we said goodbye, I thanked her for the book and told her I had enjoyed knowing her. But in truth I was relieved she was going. She would no longer be a witness to my family's peculiarities.

The new maid, Lizzie, was more the stereotype of a servant. She had a heavy Southern accent and could barely read or write. My mother said she wasn't very bright and that it was difficult to teach her how to do things, but inwardly I think my mother was pleased to feel superior once again.

My brother went away to college in the fall, and I took over his bigger room and his private phone, though I had little use for it. Mainly I continued reading novels that were recommended in *Good Reading.*

George the Arab

George Somek's parents were Egyptian, so of course all the kids in school called him the Arab. He was strong and wiry, and at fourteen already had the thin, dark outline of a mustache. George was smart and a good student and possessed a code of honorable behavior, something that my friends and I lacked and therefore resented in him. He was favored by the two ancient headmasters, Mr. Berenberg and Mr. Hall, who presided over Franklin, a tiny private school that had seen better days. Mr. Berenberg taught Latin and Greek, Mr. Hall, English literature and composition. George, along with Frenchy Alexander, who had reached full puberty at twelve and walked around with a five o'clock shadow, and Julius Spellman, a blond, plump-hipped brain, were their stars. Frenchy had a heavy accent and Julius picked his nose in class and had frequent nosebleeds, so we could dismiss them easily. But George was confident and outspoken and good at soccer and basketball.

This irritated us because we couldn't look down on him the way we did nearly everyone else, either because they were grinds or because they had weaknesses, like Paul the Geek Ginsberg who stuttered terribly and could barely read, or Herbert Hirsh, an ethereal red-haired boy, who was often found in the boiler room, where he would say with an enigmatic smile that he was looking for nickels.

George could match us physically and verbally too. Marv Stein, who assigned us nicknames and masterminded our strategy, tried to intimidate George. "I bet you stayed up all night studying," he said to him one morning before a history exam.

"That's right," George answered. "I'm not stupid like you."

Other kids would be tongue-tied when Marv ridiculed them, but George stood up to him and Marv was the one left looking foolish.

Marv knew how to get us to misbehave in class, like the time Mr. Hall, dressed as usual in his three-piece suit and high button shoes, was reading to us from *The Spectator Papers*. I had recently worked out a routine where I curled my hand at the wrist and jabbed it like a lion's paw. Marv called it fanging. Marv and I were in double seats in the front row, facing Mr. Hall's big desk and Marv whispered to me to fang Mr. Hall while he read. At first I kept my arm lower than Mr. Hall's desk. "Closer," Marv whispered. I moved my hand nearer to Mr. Hall, who continued to read. The other students laughed nervously. "Fang him, fang him," Marv kept insisting, and I came closer to Mr. Hall's head. The other kids were unable to hold back their laughter and when Mr. Hall looked up I brought my arm down as fast as I could.

"Mr. Schrader, are you making fun of me," he asked in his formal way.

I shook my head. Mr. Hall took no further action and started reading again. I actually liked and respected him, but that didn't stop me from continuing to behave badly with my friends. Often several of us came back late from lunch and limped into class, dangling an arm at the elbow, claiming we'd been hit by a car. Everyone would laugh uproariously and class would be disrupted.

The school could do little with us because they needed our tuition. We didn't know it at the time, but their finances were in terrible shape, and Mr. Hall and Mr. Berenberg were in the process of selling the school to Mr. Barnes, who taught economics and also owned a large successful summer camp.

One day a group of us returned late from lunch and stopped at the coatroom on the first floor to finish eating a box of cream puffs before going to class. After eating several apiece, there was still one left, which Marv took and stuffed into a pocket of George's leather jacket. "That'll show the Arab," he said as he mushed it around. At three o'clock dismissal we waited expectantly, watching George as he zipped up. He put his hand in his pocket, looked at it and then started to leave as if nothing had happened. "Hey, Arab, going home to study?" Marv yelled at him.

George just kept walking. We left also, disappointed. "You'd think he would have been pissed," I commented. "He's chicken," Marv said.

The next morning George arrived late and sat down without looking at anyone. At lunch when we went to the coatroom George was already standing at the door with his coat on. Marv slipped on his jacket and put his hand in his pocket. "What the hell," he said, as he shook yellow goo off his hand. "It's the same thing you put in my pocket," George said, "except I pissed in it."

Marv lunged at him but George fought back and they rolled to the floor. Everyone started yelling, and Mr. Berenberg, who had been a wrestler in college, rushed in and separated them. "What's going on?" he asked. Nobody answered, and he finally let them both go after they promised not to fight anymore.

Outside we walked to the usual diner where we ate lunch. Marv wasn't wearing his jacket, though it was cold and windy. "I didn't think the Arab had it in him," he said. After that we didn't tease George about doing his homework and being such a good student. In fact, we occasionally did some homework ourselves and, though we didn't socialize with George outside of school, we got along better with him the rest of the term.

The next year George transferred to a more rigorous and prestigious school and we drifted back to our old ways. Sometimes we'd reminisce about the time the Arab had pissed in Marv's pocket, which even Marv had to admit had taken guts. Later in the year Mr. Berenberg and Mr. Hall completed the sale of the school and retired. Mr. Barnes instituted a strict dress code and lectured us about how important a good first appearance was. We disliked him intensely, but he was a big, strong, mean-spirited man and we were afraid of him. We missed Mr. Berenberg and Mr. Hall and George. We hadn't appreciated them when they were around, and now we were stuck in a grubby success-oriented atmosphere that had no spark of lightness or fun. It was what we deserved.

Dance Party

One year my father sent me to Tony and Lucille's Dance Studio two afternoons a week after school. Dancing was the key to success in life, he told me; it would help me acquire the social graces I needed to get ahead. He didn't mention anything about working harder at school, even though I had only a seventy-four average, or anything about hard work, for that matter, though he already knew about that, having worked hard all his life. Now he was beginning to enjoy himself and thought he could teach me to also.

My instructor was Gloria, a fortyish, dark-haired, full-bodied woman who held my sweaty hand as she tried to teach me the fox trot and the rhumba. I was plump and self-conscious about the size of my chest, which looked more like a young girl's breasts. I followed Gloria's instructions woodenly, all my natural coordination and rhythm destroyed by standing next to a woman with large breasts and full red lips.

My father had already mastered the fundamentals of dancing, and with my mother attended Tony and Lucille's dance parties, where he had the opportunity to show off his moves with Lucille as his dance partner. Dancing gave my father the confidence to go to El Morocco and other nightclubs, where he met millionaires and actors and politicians. After thirty years of fourteen hours of work a day, he felt that the inner social circles of America were opening up to him.

The next year, after much protesting, I was allowed to stop taking dance lessons. My mother also stopped then, saying she was too tired to go out at night. But my father continued anyway, and graduated to the Arthur Murray Studio, where he won several gold buckles at their dance contests. He befriended other contestants who, like him, were looking for new adventures. Around then my mother had a serious operation, and went to a Florida health spa for several months. My father visited her only once. "They just sit around and talk all day," he said. "It's very boring."

With my mother at the spa and my brother away at college, I ate alone every night, served by Lizzie the maid. I had few friends, and mostly stayed home and read.

One Friday night while I was watching boxing on television my father came home with another man and two women. "This is Ted and Linda and Vickie," he said in a somewhat slurred voice. "Ted and I take dance lessons from these two wonderful ladies."

Linda was dark-haired, like my instructor Gloria, but more attractive and sophisticated looking. Vickie was a tall, statuesque blonde with a friendly smile. I turned off the television and sat with them in the living room. My father poured drinks, and he and Linda sank onto the green sofa whose arms were covered with doilies crocheted by my mother. Ted and Vickie sat in soft chairs next to me, facing the sofa. Ted asked me questions about school. He said he had a daughter my age. When they finished their drinks, my father suggested they go down the hallway to the middle bedroom where he had a portable Victrola and records. It had been my old bedroom, but I had moved into my brother's larger room at the front of the hallway when he left for college. The four of them got up. "Nice meeting you, young fella," Ted said. The women laughed and made dance moves as they walked down the hallway. I turned the TV back on.

Later when I got into bed I heard the faint sounds of music coming from the next room. Then I heard the sound of the door to my parents' bedroom at the end of the hallway slam shut. As I went to sleep I wondered why my father had brought everyone home to dance when it would have been easier to go to a club.

My mother came back a few weeks later, looking well-rested. She told me what a wonderful and enlightening time she'd had at the spa. I didn't mention anything about the dance party.

Guys and Dolls

When I was fourteen and still new to the neighborhood, a friend from school fixed me up with a bona fide nymphomaniac. It was understood that I was supposed to score with her and, on the advice of several of my classmates, I took her to an expensive movie at the Roxy Theater in midtown. Debby Snow had a muscular, sturdy look and a self-contained and distant manner that somehow matched her last name. I preferred thinner, more delicate girls like her friend Penny Schayes, who had a doll-like waist and a tiny body, except for prominently displayed large pointy breasts, but Penny was already taken by Marv Stein, the friend who had fixed me up.

Soon after Debby and I settled in our seats in the theater, I reached over her shoulder and touched her breast through her cashmere sweater, but she swatted me away. I was taken aback, since Marv had said that only a homo wouldn't be able to make out with Debby. On the other hand, I was also relieved since I wasn't particularly attracted to her. Now that I had made an honest effort, I could relax and enjoy the movie.

Afterwards I took her for sandwiches at Reuben's, a fashionable restaurant in the east Fifties. The conversation was minimal. Debby either didn't have much to say or else didn't care to share her thoughts. I watched her eat her sandwich heartily as I took small bites from mine, too nervous to swallow much. I wasn't exactly a conversationalist either. I really had no experience smooth-talking girls. My mother was the only woman I was familiar with, and she mostly shopped and cooked. When she wasn't doing that she produced tiny, intricate dolls dressed in the costumes of European countries. In Poland, she had learned to sew from her father, who specialized in *passamenterie* or braid making, supposedly for uniforms for the Czar. She created the dolls from scratch, starting with lightly colored yarn wrapped tightly around metal thread in the shape of a human figure. Then she crocheted stylish dresses with big hoops. Yarn the color of hair was attached to the head. A tiny red thread represented a mouth. Each doll had a crocheted slip and pantaloons underneath the dress, which, in a sort of perverted way, I found sexy. But this scarcely prepared me to talk to girls my own age, who were as foreign to me as my mother's dolls and their countries of origin. The idea of actually getting to know a girl and liking her and having her feel the same way about me seemed inconceivable. The only talk I ever heard about girls from my brother and from my own friends was about making out. Anything less was the sign of a sissy.

With mixed feelings I took Debby home in a cab, a little disappointed that she had pushed me away so matter of factly, but relieved that the pressure of achieving a sexual conquest had been eliminated. When Debby opened the door of her apartment and stood in the hallway, I tried to decide whether to shake her hand or just wave. But to my shock she pulled me close and jammed her tongue into my mouth, all the while rubbing her powerful body against me. I could taste the sandwich from Reuben's as she wound her tongue around mine. After about thirty seconds she pulled back abruptly, smiled, and said goodnight.

I was eager to tell my friends what had happened and to find out what it all meant, so I rushed off to the Tip Toe Inn, which was nearby, where I knew they were waiting. "You get laid?" they asked when I sat down at their table. I was too innocent and näive to lie. Marv Stein smiled and said, "She knocked your hand away in the movie, but when you got home she soul-kissed you, right?"

"How'd you know that?"

"She does that with all the guys," he said. "Soul kiss first date, titty second date."

They all laughed and I did too, and then ordered another sandwich.

Charm Bracelet

Before picking up Melissa at her house I used to stop at the cigar store at the corner of 86th Street and Broadway to buy a package of mints. I bought them as much to calm myself as I did to keep my breath fresh. Melissa and I had met at camp the past summer. I had pretended to be someone who'd had lots of experience with girls and hadn't shown much interest in her, even though I thought she was beautiful. But when we got back to the city she called to invite me to a party, and we started going out.

She lived down the block from the cigar store, on Riverside Drive, in a building that took up a whole block and had lots of entrances and elevators. The doormen got to know me and would send me up without announcing me. Her father, a big, burly man with a surprisingly thin neck, would barely grunt hello. Her mother was much friendlier and more talkative, as if she were trying to make amends for her husband's surliness.

Melissa and I would go out to the movies or to a party and then eat something at a restaurant, but all this was a prelude to necking together on the sofa in the living room before her parents came home. They liked to go to nightclubs and often stayed out late.

"Jesus, still here?" her father would say when they got back. I'd nod hello and scoot out quickly.

After a few months Melissa and I graduated from the sofa to her bedroom, and the petting became heavier and more exciting, especially since we knew her parents might come home any minute. I loved lying down next to her and maneuvering my hands under her clothing. I loved her thin waist and small breasts, and the smell of her perfume and shampoo. Her ankles were heavy, which embarrassed her, and she wore long skirts to hide them, but I didn't care. In fact I liked her ankles and everything about her. Whenever we were close I would reach out, almost unconsciously, to hold her hand or just to touch her.

As much as I wanted to, I was afraid of going all the way with her, though I think Melissa would have let me. She was more adventurous than I was, and she seemed to lose her inhibitions when we lay down together. After a while she must have realized that I didn't have as much experience as I'd made it appear. But I was afraid her parents would come home early. And I was afraid of doing something you didn't do with nice girls who lived on Riverside Drive. I had never slept with anyone or even come close to it.

One night at her house I noticed a charm bracelet on her ankle and asked where she'd gotten it. "One of the boys on the football team gave it to me," she said. "They give them to all the girls on the squad."

Melissa was a cheerleader at the private school she went to. I pretended that I didn't care and didn't mention it again. A few weeks later she told me she couldn't go out with me on a Saturday night because she was doing something with friends from school. After that we still saw each other, but I felt I was now in competition with other boys. I wanted to ask the doormen to tell me who was coming around to see her.

I was planning to take her out on her birthday, but when I phoned she told me someone else had already asked her out. I hung up angrily.

The next day she called and said her mother had come up with a solution. Her parents would take us to a nightclub the night after her birthday.

The four of us rode down in a taxi and sat at a ringside table and listened to a well-known woman jazz singer. Her father drank whiskey and said hello to acquaintances at the tables around us. Melissa and I sipped rye and ginger ale, and a photographer in a short skirt took our picture.

When we came home her parents went to their bedroom, and Melissa and I kissed on the sofa and looked out at the Palisades across the Hudson.

I knew her body by heart—the little fold of flesh near one of her elbows and her thin, delicate neck and strong shoulders. She had taken her shoes off and her legs were folded under her and, as we kissed, I noticed the charm bracelet on her ankle again. It dawned on me that Melissa and her mother felt sorry for me. I had become a charity case.

When we said goodnight at the door, I pressed against her as hard as I could until I could feel her ribs. I wanted to remember every detail of her.

We continued to go out for a while longer, but our dates became more infrequent and then stopped. Melissa had moved on. Sometimes when I was in the neighborhood I would go back to the cigar store and buy mints, pretending I was on my way to her house. But I was off to somewhere else, somewhere disappointing and sad.

The Ways of the World

Ronnie LeMay was wilder than anyone else in my class at Franklin. He walked with a strut that got him into fights. His light blue eyes often took on a wild look and he could be fearless, no matter how big the other boy was. He enjoyed fighting and beating up someone or getting beaten up himself. He also liked to run down Amsterdam Avenue, shouting, Eat me, I'm a whoopie pie! Once on 84th Street and Amsterdam he negotiated with a Puerto Rican prostitute to take five of us to her room. While one of us went in at a time, the other four stood in the hallway and peered through the glass transom at the top of the door. The woman was in her thirties. She had a sad face and red lips and kept her brassiere on the whole time. A pot of beans was on the stove, which was near her bed.

Pete Friedman was the only one who could stand up to Ronnie and quiet him down. Pete was several years older than the rest of us. By mid-afternoon he'd have a five o'clock shadow. He spoke with frequent "dem's" and "dose's" like a Damon Runyon character. His father was an executive at Ripley's, a clothing store located in a warehouse, so its motto was "low overhead and low prices." Pete usually dressed in a sport jacket, a silk shirt with cufflinks, and a bright tie fastened with a gold tie clip; we nicknamed him the Doll. He would sit in the back of the classroom and study the racing form all day. When he was asked to read out loud in class, he stammered over words of more than two syllables—no one had heard of dyslexia or learning problems at the time, so we considered him stupid. But a few years later, after dropping out of college, the Doll and an older cousin opened a discount drug store that eventually became a chain.

On weekends we drank in bars even though most of us were only fifteen. Ronnie told me he liked to sneak a shot of Jack Daniels every night from his father's liquor cabinet. It gave him a glow and helped him to go to sleep. Afterwards he would refill the bottle with water to keep his father from suspecting anything.

The first time I went drinking was at the Bretton Hall Hotel at 86th Street and Broadway. I didn't know what to order, so I just sat at the table and sipped the other boys' drinks. The combination of rye and ginger ale and gin and tonic and whiskey sours made me dizzy and I fell off my chair and rolled under the table, laughing. When we were leaving, Pete the Doll helped me up and put me in a cab.

The next time we went to the Bretton Hall the Doll taught me how to nurse a drink slowly so as not to get drunk and also to save money. By the time I went to college at the age of sixteen, I felt wise in the ways of the world.

Horace Mann

In the spring of 1950, I asked my father if I could stay back a year and transfer to the Horace Mann School. I was scheduled to enter my junior year of high school before I turned fifteen. I was baby-faced and looked about twelve or thirteen. Franklin had only twenty-one students in the whole sophomore class, most of them from families that didn't know any better than to send their sons to a place where little work was done and where at the end of each year many of the teachers left. At the time my father was struggling to become a successful dress manufacturer and he didn't understand why he should pay an additional year's tuition just because I wasn't happy.

I hoped that with the extra year I would become a better student and athlete. The boys from Horace Mann I played basketball with in Central Park seemed well coached and confident. And they talked of parties and dances on the East Side that sounded magical and exclusive, not the kind of parties I went to, with the boys sneaking drinks in the bathroom and then turning out the lights and trying to kiss the girls. The boys from Horace Mann were polite but distant, and the only way I felt I would get to become friends with them was by attending their school. But my father said no. He assumed I would appreciate what he provided: a large apartment on Central Park West, private school (even if it was second-rate), and clothing from the boys' department at Saks Fifth Avenue, which was on the same floor as Wetzel's, the custom-made clothing department where he had his own suits made. After he shopped with my brother and me, he'd go for a fitting at Wetzel's, and I would watch him self-confidently show the tailor how he wanted the seams adjusted, particularly the shoulders and back of his suit jackets, so there would be no creases.

I'm sure my father loved my brother and me, but he could relate to us only as we approached manhood. For my older brother, that meant becoming a ladies' man at a young age. My brother was dark and handsome, and by the time he was thirteen, girls were attracted to him and he was making out.

"Remember to wear rubbers," my father told me one Friday night when I left to go bowling with my friends. My first thought was to tell him it wasn't raining out, but then I understood that he meant prophylactics, like the packet of Sheiks I'd found in his closet drawer when we lived in the Heights and had filled with water and thrown out the window, like balloons.

So I didn't go to Horace Mann, assuming I could have gotten in—and I graduated at sixteen, still not shaving, looking several years younger. My high school average was low and I attended New York University, which at the time wasn't as prestigious as it is now, though it did have an interesting mix of older students on the G.I. Bill and scholarship students who were from poor families and had ambition and drive. Many of the co-eds wore high heels and makeup and tight sweaters and I couldn't take my eyes off them in class. After a disastrous freshman year, I was put on probation and had to go to summer school to improve my grades, which I did just enough to enable me to continue.

Sometimes I wonder what would have happened if I'd gone to Horace Mann, whether I would have been able to settle in and do well. I already had lost much of my confidence and assumed that the boys there were smarter than I was and possessed some kind of secret to success, the way my brother did with girls, and the way my father did in the world, the kind of secret I looked for during college and for a long time afterward.

Fear of Dying

When I was younger I could never tell anyone about my fear of dying. I was afraid of choking on food. I was afraid of tearing an artery in my neck and bleeding to death when I swung a bat. At camp during the polio epidemic in the summer of '44, I limped straight to the infirmary after I heard about it. The nurse told me I didn't have polio and scolded me for panicking.

By the time I was twelve I thought I was dying at least once a day. I'd spit saliva out into a tissue to see if I was bleeding internally. I was afraid to eat chicken because I'd swallow a bone. I didn't feel manly. My father and older brother were strong and healthy, and I couldn't compete with them.

My fears became worse at puberty. Now I had to hide my weakness from girls. By the time I was eighteen I was aware that my illnesses were in my head, but I couldn't stop them. When I went for an examination to the family doctor, I told him my symptoms. He was a decent, sympathetic man with progressive, liberal interests, and he sent me to a psychiatrist on Central Park South. This was just in time, because I had recently developed a new fear to add on to my other ones. I had read in a psychology text that fluid in the ears was what gave one the ability to maintain balance and to turn one's head. After finding this out I was unable to turn my head freely. I was due for an Army physical and was fearful of disgracing myself. I was certain that if I was drafted, I wouldn't be able to get through basic training.

So I went off, anxious but hopeful, to see Dr. Sheck in his office overlooking Central Park. He was an unsmiling, intimidating man in a bow tie, but I managed to tell him how worried I was about the draft, though I forgot to mention exactly why I was so worried.

At the end of the session he said that I sounded reasonably normal for someone my age. I felt pretty good as I left his office. I was just a regular guy, I thought, nervous about the draft, like everyone. Hey, I'm average and normal, I wanted to shout out to the passersby, but by the time I reached the subway a few blocks away I remembered about the fluid in my ears and had to hold my head stiffly to keep from falling as I walked down the stairs.

Religion

When I lived in the Heights, going to temple was the most boring thing I knew. The temple was at 187th Street and Fort Washington Avenue, along a flight of stairs down the long row of steps that led to Bennett Avenue. It had a corrugated metal ceiling and was dark and gloomy. My friends and I would twist and turn all morning on the wooden benches during holidays like Yom Kippur until our parents would allow us to leave and we'd spend the rest of the day in Fort Tryon Park, with its carefully tended flowers and raised benches from which we could glimpse the Hudson River. Once on Yom Kippur some gentile boys waited at the top of the steps and offered us BLT sandwiches, which we refused. Eating bacon publicly seemed too sinful on such a high holiday.

The male worshippers, wrapped in their long tallises, moved strangely back and forth as they davened. Occasionally someone fainted. The most religious person in our family was Hymie, who was married to my great-aunt Hannie. Hymie spent every Saturday in temple praying vigorously. He also beat his three sons. At his death none of them came to his funeral, but that was much later. When she was in her seventies, Aunt Hannie complained to the family doctor that Hymie still bothered her every night, and the doctor reprimanded him. "If I don't bother my wife," Hymie answered, "who should I bother then?"

I didn't do well in my bar mitzvah preparations, so it was postponed several months until December. My father hired Aaron, a young bearded rabbinical student, to supplement my regular studies. Aaron turned out to be the first good teacher I'd ever had, religious or secular. He made everything clear and interesting. He showed me that, as a lefty, my handwriting would be much better in Hebrew than in English because Hebrew started from the right side and I didn't have to curl my wrist awkwardly as I did when writing English. Soon I was printing neat Hebrew letters. Aaron looked at the class picture from Franklin and pointed out who the best students were and who were the most vacant-minded. To me, it seemed like a miracle that he could guess so accurately. I still don't know how he did it.

Thanksgiving weekend, three weeks before my bar mitzvah, I fractured my elbow running into a fence while playing basketball. My friends took me to St. Elizabeth's Hospital, which was a half block away, and the nuns placed me on a bed in the emergency room. I kicked the walls in pain, despite the nuns' insistence that I lie still, and my sneakers left black marks. When my mother arrived, she arranged for an ambulance to take us to Beth Israel Hospital where our regular physician practiced. A specialist, Arthur Barsky, set my elbow and put it in a cast. Later, during the Fifties, he and his brother Edward lost their positions at the hospital because they wouldn't reveal the names of people who had given money to send volunteer physicians to the Spanish Civil War.

My cast was removed a few days before my bar mitzvah and at the party I tried not to wince in pain as people handed me envelopes with checks and squeezed my arm. I managed to recite my haftorah portion without too many errors, a tribute to Aaron's pedagogy, but that was one of the last times I attended temple. In the spring we moved downtown and stopped going, even on high holidays. In the Heights we knew everyone, but downtown no one seemed to care what you did, including the neighbors in our building on Central Park West.

My inclination was to become an atheist, but since I couldn't satisfactorily explain the world's existence, I considered myself an agnostic. One thing I was certain of was that the God I had been told about in temple could not have been the one who started everything. He was too mean-spirited and lacked imagination. To try and understand life, I began reading the paperback novels I found at downtown bookstores. I read books like *Knock on Any Door* by Willard Motley, with its epigraph, "Live fast, die young, and have a good-looking corpse," and James Jones' *From Here to Eternity*, melodramatic novels with characters who led exciting lives and experienced much pain and pleasure. I stayed up late at night, reading and eating pints of ice cream until my mind and tongue were raw. Some days I remained home from school, pretending to be sick so I could keep reading.

It wasn't until my junior year at New York University that I found English courses that encouraged me to read literature, something I had until then considered private and almost sinful.

On Yom Kippur of my senior year I planned to go to N.Y.U. as usual, having sworn never to cut class again after all my hooky-playing in high school. I put on my usual khakis and sweatshirt and started to leave. My father was at the door in a suit and tie and a fedora, waiting for one of his friends to pick him up so they could drive to the racetrack. He asked me to put on something more presentable. "It's a Jewish holiday," he said. "It doesn't look nice."

I said something about not being a hypocrite and gathered up my notebook and the novel I was studying and headed for the subway.

Part III The Young Writer

The Young Writer

After my junior year in college, I spent the summer in the house my parents had rented at Atlantic Beach, reading and trying to write short stories. I felt unable to compete with my father's success in the dress business. The only path open to me was to become a famous writer. I had taken a writing class that year, and a story of mine about an exhibition diver in a Florida hotel had just come out in *The Apprentice*, the N.Y.U. literary magazine. My stories were about tortured young people trying to find themselves in a crass, materialistic world, which was how I saw my own life. The main character in "The Diver" is a young woman who rebels against her mother's attempt to marry her off to someone rich. She identifies with the diver, who seems fresh and pure to her. At the conclusion of the story the diver hits his head against the diving board at the hotel pool while attempting a dive, and the young woman runs away toward the ocean.

In the real world I felt incompetent and a failure. My mother, to whom I showed my stories, always said something like, that's nice but will you be able to make a living from it? I should have tried to get a job or traveled somewhere, but at nineteen I had no confidence in myself and little independence. I was moody and over-sensitive, and my father didn't know what to make of me and kept his distance. At my age he had already run away from the Polish army and lived in two countries on his own and was about to arrive with no money in the United States. He looked on his success with great pride and assumed I would, too. But his money only made me feel ashamed of having life so easy. I was critical of him and of business, but I wasn't able to think of what I might aim to do in the world that would be helpful and rewarding.

Atlantic Beach at that time was a small community of renters from New York City and local people who had done well, along with a smattering of gangsters with big shiny cars parked in their driveways. The blocks were arranged alphabetically. We were on Erie Street in a large house next to Willy Klein, a friend of my father's who was in women's coats. All of my father's friends worked in some aspect of women's clothing—furs, jewelry, perfumes, shoes. After my mother read my story in the magazine, she mentioned it to my father. That evening after dinner, right before his friends began arriving for the weekly poker game, my father told me he'd like to read it. I barely had time to show him the magazine before the card players began coming in. Willy shook my hand and poked me in the stomach. "You must be having some time with the girls, a good-looking kid like you," he said. "I wish I was your age again."

I nodded my head and blushed. "You're talking to a published writer," my father said. "Another Tolstoy." He held up the magazine. "Let's hear it," Willy said. By this time six of my father's friends were sitting at the round poker table with its green felt top, drinking Scotch. At first I said I couldn't but my father handed me the magazine. "Read it," he commanded, and I began in a quivering voice.

Everyone sat quietly and respectfully while I read and when I finished they burst into applause. "Bravo," Willy said. My father said he was proud of me as he began to deal the first hand. I said goodnight, elated but also confused. How could they praise a story so critical of the way they led their lives?

Failed Romances

Sarah Weinstein had a bohemian look that made her popular. Dark hair pulled back in a ponytail, no makeup, sandals. My friend Ben told me he and everyone else had a crush on her and invited me to his American Lit class to take a look. Ben was a top student, wrote for the N.Y.U. paper, and was a hard-working, socially conscious individual. But he was a little earnest then, and it wasn't until years later that he added a few pounds to his scrawny frame, had his teeth straightened, and became a charming, sophisticated professor. So I was the one who ended up with Sarah.

In June I spent a week at her parents' house in Maine instead of attending my graduation. Sarah still had another year left. Her parents were sophisticated German Jews who traveled in intellectual circles. Their house in Maine was tasteful and beautiful, and I enjoyed driving around the island with Sarah and going to deserted beaches and later listening to classical music on their wonderful hi-fi equipment, but the sex between us was disappointing. Sarah had hung around the Village as a teenager, and she and several of her friends had been deflowered at fifteen by a sandal maker who lived above his sandal store and serviced young girls who came to the Village. He also gave them all crabs.

When we got into bed the first night, Sarah took out her diaphragm and found a note from her mother telling her that it had a hole in it. I was shocked that her mother knew about her diaphragm. I had never seen one before. Sarah told me I should withdraw before climaxing and I nodded as if this was routine behavior for me, which it definitely wasn't. I had never spent a whole night with a woman. Most of my sexual experience was limited to a couple of times in the front seat of a car with a girl from South Orange, New Jersey, where all the while I had to keep my eye out for the police, who periodically chased cars from the parking lot we used.

Before I went to bed I showered, shaved, and combed my hair. "You got all fixed up," Sarah said. I grinned sheepishly.

Intercourse with Sarah was over almost before it began. I had been thinking about this moment all day and I had to pull out in about thirty seconds. Sarah patted my shoulder, turned on her side and went to sleep. I kept pressing against her and touching her but she slept through it. And that was pretty much the story every night when we had sex. I was horny the whole time, but Sarah didn't seem too interested. I figured there was something wrong with me and was too embarrassed to say anything.

When we got back to the city Sarah went to summer school and pretty much dropped me. "I get intense about things," she told me when I pleaded to see her. "And right now I'm pretty intense about French Literature."

Twelve years later I met her at Fire Island where she was visiting a friend. She was married to an ophthalmologist in Washington, D.C., and had three children. She looked the same—ponytail, no makeup—and we chatted on the beach. She seemed more ordinary now—it was the late Sixties and lots of women had adopted her look. She told me about the joys and difficulties of raising her three children. I didn't mention our trip to Maine, though it passed through my mind as we talked. After a while we shook hands and said goodbye.

Marisol was someone I also met in my senior year in college. We sat next to one another in an introductory science class that I needed in order to graduate. She was a freshman, obviously bright, and a good student. She was sweet and attractive, a little chubby, not the kind of hard-edged femme fatale I was looking for. We chatted before class and studied together in the student lounge for the final. I had the feeling she liked me, but it wasn't until two years later when I was in the Army at Fort Dix, New Jersey, that I found her number in my phone book and called her up. I had backed out of getting married a few months before, and after a long depression, Marisol was the first woman I called for a date. Her parents were from Spain and she lived with them in Yonkers in a small white house that had a Spanish-looking garden in the back. Her mother and father were cultivated and charming, but I think she was a little impatient with their old world ways.

I took her to the Bronx Botanical Gardens on a Sunday afternoon and we ended up sitting on a grassy hill near rows of brightly colored flowers. Marisol leaned close and turned her head toward me, clearly wanting me to kiss her. An old woman in a canvas chair about thirty feet away looked at us with disapproval, which inhibited me. I felt awkward being with someone after all my months of moping around. And, though I liked Marisol, she seemed more like a friend than someone to go out with. So we sat on the grass and talked until the sun started to go down. The moment had passed. I went back to Fort Dix and forgot about her. The next year when I got out of the Army and was feeling better, I remembered her and realized that I wanted to see her. When I called, her father told me she was at graduate school in Chicago. He didn't sound happy about it and said he missed her. I told him I did too.

Something to Do

A friend used to say that it was harder to get things done when you had too much time on your hands. If you weren't working, for instance, it was difficult simply to get your clothes to the laundromat. You might, in fact, build the whole day around bringing in your wash. But if you had a job you'd just carry it in on the way to work and pick it up later on the way home, a footnote in the day's routine.

This friend's name was Mendy. He was thin and handsome, and had an ironic sense of humor and a sophistication that I hadn't run into before. He lived in the West Village in a picturesque apartment that had a slanted wooden floor like a Van Gogh painting. Mendy had been a graduate student in psychology at the University of Michigan, but had transferred to City College, where he also had a part-time job on a research project. I had met him at the University of Michigan, where I spent a semester in the graduate writing program before dropping out. Now I was living at home on Central Park West, looking for a job connected in some way to writing and planning to move to my own place.

Mendy introduced me to marijuana, which he smoked frequently and which I pretended to enjoy. He knew about drugs like LSD, which was just coming into vogue, and peyote, which I had heard was used by the Hopi Indians as part of their religion. Mendy told me about the Tropical Plant Company in Laredo, Texas, which for ten dollars would send you a bunch of small peyote plants in the mail. I sent a check and when the package arrived I brought it to Mendy's apartment. He sliced each cactus plant into thin pieces, which he hung on metal hangers to dry on his fire escape. A few days later he ground them with a blender and put the powder into capsules, which we divided between us. Then we each swallowed a few and went to a party. But I felt dizzy, as if I'd had too much to drink, and went home. I was disappointed that I hadn't seen visions the way I'd heard the Hopis did.

A few weeks later I was home alone on a bright Sunday morning. My parents were away for the weekend and I swallowed about eight pills, or buttons, as Mendy called them. This time they worked. Rays of sunshine took on rainbow hues as they shone through the Venetian blinds. The flush of a toilet changed into the chords of a Beethoven symphony. This lasted through the afternoon, and by early evening I was tired of the colors and hallucinations that had been bombarding me for hours.

I was twenty-one years old and had spent a beautiful summer day indoors by myself. I was hungry and lonely, so I took the subway downtown to the Village and went to the Limelight, a large popular coffee house where Mendy usually hung out. He was at a table with a group of friends and I joined them and ordered a bottle of beer and a steak and told everybody about taking peyote that morning. Usually I was shy, but this time I had something to talk about. By now my visions had slowed down, and if I closed my eyes I saw cartoon figures like Mickey Mouse, which I described to everyone. Mendy joked about peyote revealing the inner person, which in my case was someone who saw cartoons. I laughed along with everyone else, just happy to be connecting with other people. They were classmates of Mendy's from City College, and they seemed bright and interesting. Jean, the woman next to me, had long reddish brown hair and I found her attractive, but I felt too shy to say much to her because I assumed she was the girlfriend of one of the men at the table.

About a month later Mendy became ill and found out that he had cancer. He started going for chemotherapy and I talked with him about moving in to help him manage, but before we could make arrangements he went into the hospital and, a few weeks later, died.

Jean called to tell me that the funeral was in the Bronx on the Grand

Concourse. Afterwards a bunch of us went for coffee and bagels a few blocks away at Jean's parents' place. I wanted to ask whether Mendy's apartment was available, but I felt that would be in bad taste, so I said nothing. But when I left I did manage to ask Jean for her number, and she seemed happy to give it to me.

Mendy was dead and I was still living with my parents, but at least I had something to do.

Chinese Laundry

Soon after my family moved to Central Park West, I started taking my shirts to the Chinese laundry down the block on Columbus Avenue and 76th Street. The man behind the counter would always say, "Hello, boy," when I came in. He spoke with a heavy accent, the kind my friends and I used when we told a joke involving someone Chinese, with punch lines like, "No tickee, no shirtee." I didn't give the man a thought and wouldn't have been able to pick him out in a lineup of other Chinese men, since they all looked the same to me.

Within a few years the laundry closed, and I found another a few blocks away. When I was twenty-one I started working for my father in the dress business and moved to a friend's apartment on 54th Street. People at work called me Mr. Schrader and deferred to me in conversation. Looking at myself in the showroom mirrors, I saw a future industry leader. One morning on the way to work, I brought my shirts into the laundry around the corner between Seventh Avenue and Broadway. The man behind the counter looked at me closely and asked, "You boy?"

He was a thin, slightly balding Chinese man in his early fifties. I didn't recognize his face, but I knew his voice. "You must be from 76th Street," I said. He nodded his head and smiled. Every time I came in after that he'd smile and say, "Hello, boy," and I'd smile back, though I wasn't sure I liked being called boy anymore.

One morning I woke up and discovered I had no clean shirts and rushed down to the store. My laundry was due to be ready that day, but when I held out the ticket the man said, "Ready later."

"But I need them now. They're supposed to be ready today."

"Shirts ready later," he repeated.

"Damn," I said. I slammed the door on the way out and returned home and put on the shirt I had worn the day before. At the end of work that evening I came back to the store to try again. The man didn't say anything as he took my ticket and reached for my package of shirts on the shelf behind him. After that he stopped calling me boy.

Dress Salesman

I had gone to work for my father so that I could get to know him better and perhaps to earn some respect from him. I felt the same way about my brother, who already had his own division in the company. Both of them had always seemed like business types. I was known as the dreamer.

It didn't help that I couldn't stand the dresses my father's company made, dresses to go to work in or to wear to cocktail parties. The young women I knew wore jeans and sweatshirts. But I was hopeful of proving myself, and watched the other salesmen hold up dresses and guarantee re-orders. I learned terms like "mother of the bride" and "Peter Pan collar" and "paisley print."

The salesmen were all outgoing and dynamic personalities. They flirted with the store buyers and did cha-cha moves as they displayed a dress. They were entertainers, and would say anything to make a sale. I watched one of them jump onto a table where buyers were sitting and hold up a dress, and shout, "You gotta take it, you gotta take it!"

I studied the tags on the dresses to learn prices and sizing and delivery dates. I memorized how well they were selling. But I didn't feel ready to stand in front of a buyer and sell. Finally, on a slow day, the sales director told me the next buyer was mine. She was a kindly looking older woman from Asheville, North Carolina, with blue-grey hair. When she asked me how a dress I was showing her was doing, I said it was the twenty-seventh best seller on the line. She looked at me with a puzzled expression and said she would pass on it.

Out of the corner of my eye I could see the other salesmen trying to contain their laughter. I was in the wrong business.

Wholesale

One day my friend Lenny asked if his girlfriend could buy something wholesale. Lenny was writing a novel and living with Elinor, a recent graduate of Smith. She was bright and sophisticated, already an assistant producer for CBS, and she wanted to buy a dress wholesale as much for the adventure as for the savings. I turned her over to Seymour, a salesman who often worked in the stockroom with small stores. Seymour was wiry, with a thick brown mustache that gave him a slightly weaselly look. He was, like most of the other salesmen in their late thirties, reasonably intelligent, but from a poor family. He had been forced to go to work after high school and then drafted into the army during the Second World War. When he was discharged, he married his girlfriend and had children, and was now a salesman for life. Seymour took whatever perks he could get from his job, so when Elinor walked down the stockroom aisle he followed her and rubbed his hand on her backside. Elinor pushed him away several times, until he stopped. Then, as if nothing had happened, she resumed looking at dresses. Lenny called later and joked about what he labeled Elinor's Seventh Avenue experience. He said he might use it in his novel.

The next week Elinor's best friend, Julia, asked if she could come up also. Julia was a classmate of Elinor's. She was a brunette with large lips and an innocent but sultry look that resembled Brigitte Bardot. Men were always coming onto her in the street. She refused their offers and suggestions with a polite "No thank you." I turned her over to Seymour, telling him she was a friend of Elinor's.

But when Julia started looking at dresses, Seymour kept his distance. Perhaps he'd already had enough of college girls with Elinor, or maybe Julia's obvious sexiness was too intimidating. After a few minutes Julia chose a dress and handed it to him. "Seymour," she asked, "aren't you going to feel me up the way you did with Elinor?" Seymour shook his head, confused. He was the one who was supposed to be the aggressor. When she left, Seymour told me that in the future he'd prefer not to take care of my friends.

Victor

Like Seymour, most of the dress salesmen had their little idiosyncrasies. Freddie compulsively rearranged the samples on the rack in the showroom all day. Victor, who was a bright, energetic balding man, constantly paced around the showroom like a caged animal and rushed downstairs on errands once or twice a day. He lived on Long Island with his wife. His daughter was studying for her Ph.D. in art history. Victor was quick and impulsive, and liked making deals with buyers.

Six months after Victor began working at the firm, dresses began to disappear. No one could understand it. Manny, the head of shipping, had worked at the company since he was sixteen, with time off for the Army in the Second World War, and he knew all the angles. But every month the inventory was ten or twenty dresses short. Manny told Harriet, who was in charge of the stockroom, to keep an eye on some of the local small store owners who came in for specials and liked to sneak dresses into their shopping bags or under their skirts.

One morning Manny saw Victor rush out of the showroom and decided to follow him. He took the next elevator down and spotted Victor walking north on Seventh Avenue toward 40th Street. Victor turned west at the corner and walked quickly, with Manny a short distance behind, to the Port Authority Building on Eighth. He went straight to the storage lockers, inserted a coin and took the key out. He pulled out a dress from under his coat, placed it in the locker, and closed it shut with the key, which he put in his coat pocket. Then he rushed back to the showroom. Manny returned a few minutes later, went to the coat closet in the back, and took the key from Victor's coat.

Then he walked back to the Port Authority Building and removed the dress from the locker. He left an unsigned note telling Victor he'd been discovered. Then he returned the key to Victor's pocket and explained to the owner of the company what he'd done. Stealing wasn't uncommon: the year before the piece goods man had stolen thousands of dollars of fabric by falsifying invoices; truckers always tried to skim dresses from their deliveries.

Victor rushed out at five as usual, but he was back in fifteen minutes, looking pale. Manny was waiting with the boss. Victor apologized and told them he'd stolen dresses for his girlfriend and promised it would never happen again. The boss didn't contradict him, even though he was certain Victor had been selling the dresses, and he agreed to give him another chance.

After that Victor stopped rushing out of the showroom during the day, but he seemed to lose his energy and enthusiasm, and a few months later he left for another job. When the new company called for a reference, the boss didn't mention Victor's stealing.

Business Friends

After my father first succeeded as a dress manufacturer, he gained the confidence to come out from the back where production and shipping were done and walk into the showroom and meet the buyers from around the country who were ordering his dresses. For over twenty years previously he'd been a dress contractor, the one who sewed the dresses for the manufacturer, which meant going through back doors and begging for work. But now my father, who was five foot five and spoke with an accent, no longer felt like an outsider. He started dressing in custom-made clothing, offering buyers drinks in his office and taking them out to dinner and to nightclubs. Though most of them were born in America and weren't Jewish, he managed to forge friendships based on a shared desire to make money and enjoy the good life.

One of his favorite buyers was Edie Cranston from Charles Stevens, a large department store in Chicago. She was a tiny elderly widow with an appetite for life equal to my father's. At dinner she was able to match him drink for drink. When she was in New York for market week, he would take her out to dinner on several nights, and when he visited Chicago he would go out with her and her son Chip, who was a Navy pilot. My father gave her presents and spoke to her frequently on the phone. In return, she placed enormous orders. "She's something," my father would say. "She must have a wooden leg the way she drinks." They did business profitably together for around fifteen years until she retired. After she left the store, Freddy Breit, the Midwest salesman, would phone her whenever he was in Chicago. She told him that she was doing fine and that her son was now married and a father. The only thing that disappointed her was that my father had never called to say hello after her retirement. When Freddy told me this I mentioned it to my father, thinking he'd call. "Is she crazy?" my father said. "She was great when she had a pencil. I was good to her, took her out, shmeared her plenty. But now, forget it. What can she do for me?"

I felt bad for her. And I felt bad for my father, too, that he was so cold about people and business.

Living in Bill Cole's Apartment

In the spring of 1957 I rented a room on West 54th Street in the apartment of Bill Cole, after I'd met him through a woman I took out a few times. I was twenty-one, a year out of college, and unhappy working in the dress business. The apartment was a little musty—the walls were filled with books, and the furniture sagged—but it was spacious and bright. Bill was in his late thirties, tall and handsome. He had grown up on Staten Island, been drafted into the Second World War straight out of high school, and stationed in England. After his discharge he became the publicity director at Knopf, at the time one of the most prestigious independent publishers in the country. When I met him he was divorced, with two daughters who lived in New Jersey with their mother. Between his own expenses and child support payments, Bill had little money, but while I was there we had many dinner parties attended by friends and young women passing through New York who'd been given Bill's number by mutual friends. One of these young women, Marny, supposedly Robert Graves' mistress in Majorca, asked if she could take a bath when she first came to the apartment because she found the air in New York so dirty. Then she emerged from the bathroom wrapped in a towel and had a drink.

Bill didn't like to sleep alone and kept a list of about twelve women he could count on spending the night with. He listed them in preference from one to twelve, but even number twelve, who wasn't a great beauty, was lively and the two of them seemed to enjoy themselves whenever she stayed over. Bill's behavior shocked me. I wanted to go out only with women I was in love with. Of course these women were usually in love with someone else and weren't interested in me. I was attracted to thin, nervous types who resembled my mother, though I didn't realize that at the time.

So I watched Bill's life, both fascinated and repelled, though I had to admit his dinner parties were great fun. Bill taught me how to make a salad—wash the lettuce and then dry it on paper towels, and mix the dressing with oil and vinegar and lots of garlic, salt and pepper. The only salad dressings I had seen until then came out of a bottle. Bill prepared dinner while drinking Scotch and singing Irish and English folk songs. He loved poetry, occasionally wrote light verse, and edited many anthologies of poetry and cartoons. His parties were attended by young writers and cartoonists, along with editors. I met James Baldwin, a Knopf author, and Philip Roth, whom Bill introduced to me as a Jewish writer, which I thought meant he wrote in Yiddish. I also met young cartoonists like Jules Feiffer, Shel Silverstein, and Herb Gardner, who later wrote the play *A Thousand Clowns*, but was known then as the creator of the Nebbish, a Sad Sack character merchandised on cups and other household items.

And I met André Françoise, an incredibly handsome Frenchman who was forty-two and made me think that forty-two must be the handsomest age there was. Women dangled their keys in front of him to entice him home with them, but as far as I could tell he was faithful to his wife in Paris. His drawings had an original and often scatological point of view. In one of them a kindly looking old woman in a rocking chair was crocheting a giant penis. But though I found the atmosphere exciting, I thought of Bill's life as superficial. Too many parties and girlfriends, and too much liquor, and too much gossip disguised as literary talk.

One night at dinner in the apartment I sat next to Jeannine, an attractive Swiss woman who was in New York for a few weeks. She ended up staying with me that night. Jeannine was engaged to someone in Geneva but wanted a last fling in New York before settling down. In the morning I told her I wanted to see her exclusively while she was in the city but she refused, and I said I couldn't accept that. "You Americans are such children," she told me.

Another time I took out a sixteen-year-old girl from Guatemala, who had come to help her sister take care of a new baby. Her sister was married to a friend of my brother's. Marie was tall and stunning and spoke little English. She seemed excited to meet me and to be in an apartment that overlooked Times Square. I had the feeling this was the first time she had been out of her sister's apartment in Queens. Bill joined my brother's friend and me and Marie and her sister for drinks, and sang a few lines of a Spanish folk song, which pleased the two young women. Later the four of us had dinner at an Italian restaurant and then took a ride on the Staten Island ferry. Marie and I walked to the upper deck and stared at the skyline of New York. She leaned against me and smiled and held my hand and guided it onto her breast. I could feel her heart beating under her sweater. We kissed for a long time. Yet even as we kissed, I started thinking that Marie was somehow trying to trap me into marriage, the way I imagined her sister might have trapped my brother's friend. Her sister was plain looking and seemed tired and cranky from having recently given birth. I wondered if that was how Marie would look eventually. The next morning Bill told me what a beauty she was. "A ripe young peach," he said, "there for the taking." But I never called her.

After I had been in the apartment for a year I received notification from the Army that I could expect to be drafted immediately. I decided to move home and arranged for Stan, a friend of mine, to take my place. Bill asked me to help him give one last party before I left. He wanted to thank a number of writers and editors who had been helpful to him over the past year and he felt the best way was to invite them to a party with attractive women. Bill calculated that if he, Stan, Alex (a former roommate), and I each invited the five best-looking women we knew, we would start with a roomful of knockouts. We bought several bottles of Jack Daniels. Alex chose some cheap wine, the kind he usually brought to dinner. Later he became a well-known wine critic, but at the time he didn't care how it tasted. Bill added pretzels, potato chips, cheese and crackers.

Bill's friends, most of them sophisticated, older men, seemed pleased to be surrounded by young, lively women. Someone introduced himself to me as William Styron, but he said it in such an ironic, caustic way that I wasn't sure if he was kidding or not. He might have used the same tone to tell me he was Ernest Hemingway. Philip Roth kept saying he ought to leave soon because he had to get up early to write the next morning, but he showed no sign of leaving. I'm sure I had many other conversations but they all blend into a blurred memory of older men laughing and drinking and talking to younger women. Gene, the super of the building, was there. He was a black man who liked to party and drink the way Bill did, and they had become great friends. And Pierre, another former roommate of Bill's, was also there. Pierre was the stereotypical Frenchman, preoccupied with women. Tall and handsome, with a big, foolish grin, his conversation was peppered with ooh-la-la's. His usual method on a date after entering a woman's apartment, he told me, was to try to kiss her. "Mostly I get slapped," he said in a heavy accent, "but sometimes it works and then, ooh-la-la." He cruised around the party shaking his head in disbelief and taking down numbers in his black book.

I stood against the wall with Natalie, one of the women I had invited. She was a recent Sarah Lawrence graduate, bright and lively, whom I had gone out with several times. She kept holding my hand and nuzzling against me. But I was beyond sexual interest. I was witnessing the unfolding of a work of art, which I had helped create and I wanted to enjoy it undividedly. Miraculously, around midnight more beautiful women arrived, members of the chorus line of *Flower Drum Song*, which was playing at a nearby theater. Somehow they had heard about the party and rushed over at the end of the show. I saw Roth shake his head and give up all pretense of leaving. Pierre's face was frozen in a dazed smile, his black book put away. I leaned against the wall and held Natalie's hand.

The party lasted until two thirty. I took Natalie home and gave her a quick, goodnight kiss. I wanted to get back to the apartment and bask in whatever atmosphere and electricity was left. The next morning I had coffee with Bill and the woman who had stayed—I don't remember what number she was on his list. We cleaned up and talked about the party. Even Bill was awestruck. Later he was inspired to bang away at his typewriter for an hour or two, which he occasionally did on weekends.

I moved out soon after and stopped working, but I wasn't drafted until six months later. I exercised every day to get in shape for basic training, but time passed slowly. Life at home seemed lonely and empty, and I often thought of all the beautiful women at the party whose numbers I hadn't gotten.

Sex Without Guilt

When I was twenty-two, I fell in love with someone who, as usual, didn't return my feelings. I first met Alda through a friend, a woman who was going out with a writer from *The Village Voice*, which was then a new and adventurous publication. Alda had dirty blonde hair and a sturdy body, was lively and often said outrageous things. When I took her to dinner on St. Patrick's Day at an Italian restaurant on Thompson Street, where they played bocce ball in the back, she asked the couple at the next table if their green pitcher of beer would make them pee green. I was embarrassed but also in awe. She talked openly of sex and nearly anything else that came to her mind, and seemed to lack the inward censor that everyone else appeared to have. Alda was a year younger than I was and came from a working class family in New Jersey. She'd arrived in New York after high school and taken a job as a secretary, and was an evening student at New York University. The previous year, she told me, she and a boyfriend would have sex before her class at N.Y.U. and then she'd go straight to college without washing so the professor and the other students could smell the after-sex on her and feel envious. This was in 1957, when even bohemians tended to still wear ties and jackets.

I laughed knowingly at Alda's jokes and confessions. I was shocked, of course, but I was also smitten. One day I took her to Long Beach, Long Island, and as we stared out at the ocean, suggested we become a couple. "You're too young, too innocent," she said. "I like older men, usually on the nasty side." She described going to bed with one of the owners of the *Village Voice*, a plump bearded man who had an apartment on Christopher Street near the *Voice* office, where people connected to the paper had informal spaghetti dinners and wine, and where I'd first met Alda. She said that she'd gone to bed with him one night and that in the middle of intercourse he'd reached for a glass tube on a table next to the bed and inserted it into her vagina. "Isn't that great?" he said.

I used to go to the Limelight coffee house in the evening and look for people I knew. In a back room it had what was then one of the first photography galleries. The Limelight was owned by Helen Gee, an attractive blonde who was divorced from a Chinese man and sometimes went out with my roommate Bill.

"Everyone seems to be getting laid except me," I told Alda one night at the Limelight in a last plea to get her to change her mind, but she turned me down gently. "I've got someone new," she said. "My former shrink, Albert Ellis." I'd heard of him, of course. He wrote best sellers like *Sex Without Guilt*, manuals telling people how to be free and abandoned and to escape from feeling guilty about their freedom. Alda had been his patient the year before and had propositioned him after a couple of sessions, but Ellis told her there had to be a year's interval before anything sexual could occur between him and a former patient. Alda immediately stopped seeing him and now the year was up. Ellis had offered to set her up in an apartment near his office on 57th Street and pay for her to study photography. In return she was to make dinner for him at ten or eleven, when he finished seeing patients. Alda accepted enthusiastically; photography was her love and she enjoyed cooking, and the late night sex was fine too. She invited me over to dinner the next week at ten.

Though I was disappointed at Alda's turndown, I was excited to meet someone as famous as Albert Ellis. Alda introduced him to me as Al and we shook hands. He was tall and handsome and reminded me of photos of Arthur Miller. I told him I knew very little about psychology, though I was interested. "Go ahead," he said. "Shoot away. I love talking about it." At dinner I asked him questions ranging from how to choose a therapist to the definition of popular terms like other-directed. He answered clearly and at length. I was flattered and kept coming up with more questions and comments. We were talking as equals, or at least I, as a neophyte, was being taken seriously. This was the way to learn things, I thought. In college my mind had always drifted to daydreams about the women in class during a professor's lectures. But with the intense interaction at dinner I felt I was getting a year's worth of Psychology 1, and more. My head was spinning in excitement with the nuances of psychological insight. When I left, I thanked Alda for inviting me, and told Ellis how much I had enjoyed talking with him.

The next day I called Alda to thank her again and tell her how flattered I was by Ellis' attention.

"Well, he did have an ulterior motive," Alda told me. "He's always working. His tape recorder was on last night all through dinner. He told me you were the perfect layman. You asked him lots of basic questions that he'll be able to use and expand on."

I was shocked. All that attention hadn't been based on my promise and intelligence, but instead on my ordinariness. I was Everyman, the typical dolt who bought his books, someone to be observed and prodded. I was too innocent for Alda but just innocent enough for Ellis.

That was the last time I spoke with her. Later I went into psychotherapy, but I don't think it helped much. I heard Ellis married and continued a long successful career and is still practicing into his nineties.

My Life and Philip Roth

In 1959, while I was in the Army at Fort Dix, I dated Mendy's old friend Jean, who lived on the outskirts of the East Village on Stuyvesant Street, a tiny block between Third and Second Avenue, that ran at an angle to Ninth Street. She had a small apartment in a brownstone near Third with high ceilings and big windows that looked out on a pleasant view with trees. She worked as a freelance copy editor and was quiet and dreamy and had a good sense of humor and knew lots of painters and writers. Once we went to a loft party and watched Allen Ginsberg dance with a man, which, in my innocence, I found shocking. At another party on West 25th Street, a man who'd been drinking too much fell twenty feet onto the roof of a neighboring building. "I've got pot on me," someone said and ran out. Most everyone else did too. I also decided to leave since I had come home on a weekend pass and was afraid I'd get in trouble. But I felt bad leaving someone seriously injured. Later I found out that the man had been quite drunk, and landed so softly he hadn't broken any bones. He was released from the hospital the next day. Life seemed full of surprises.

Jean took me to the Cedar Bar and the White Horse, which were the places to go at the time. I wouldn't have frequented either of them myself, but Jean knew her way around and I felt comfortable with her. I began spending weekends at her place on Stuyvesant Street. Philip Roth lived down the block near Second Avenue. I knew him from a few parties; he had a quick sense of humor and I had enjoyed talking to him. He had just started publishing stories and wasn't famous yet. One Saturday morning Jean and I ran into him while we were walking to the laundromat. He told me he'd been in the Army a few years before in Washington, D.C., and had written movie reviews in his spare time. I knew he was a published writer and I was proud to stand there with Jean and chat with him, but I also felt we were more or less equal. He was a year or two older and I hadn't published or written much, but I planned to catch up to him. Recently a piece of mine had come out in an anthology for college freshmen edited by one of my professors from N.Y.U. In the table of contents it was listed between Ben Franklin and John Ruskin, and had squeezed out one of the greatest personal essays of the 20th century, Orwell's "Shooting an Elephant," which was discarded because the publisher, McGraw-Hill, wanted new and unknown essays, rather than familiar ones.

Roth pointed out his first floor apartment to us. There were steps leading down so you could see in through the window, and a number of times over the next few months I glimpsed him in his shorts, typing away furiously. A year later he won the National Book Award for his first book, *Goodbye, Columbus*. I was still at Fort Dix, a company clerk with almost a year left to serve.

By then I wasn't seeing Jean any more. She had wanted to get married and at first I tentatively agreed. Almost before I knew it I met her parents, and Jean and I were arguing about whom to invite to the wedding. I went berserk when she suggested an old lover of hers. I hadn't minded him before, but all of a sudden getting married changed everything. Her parents reserved a reception room at the Plaza Hotel. Jean shopped for a white gown. She gave up her place on Stuyvesant Street and we searched for an apartment near Fort Dix. A few times we stayed at my parents' apartment on weekends, and my mother was upset that Jean liked to sleep until noon. "There's something wrong with her," she said to me, putting more doubt in my mind about getting married.

I hated talking about the wedding. When I was with Jean, all I wanted to do was have sex. I'd touch her under her dress or place her hand between my legs as we sped around New Jersey on weekends searching for a place to live. I half hoped to die in a crash and not have to get married. I didn't know how to back out. I felt paralyzed. Writing, all of a sudden, like Philip Roth with his National Book Award, seemed beyond me. The thought of standing up in a tuxedo in front of a hundred and fifty people terrified me. I was a clerk in the Army and had no idea what I was going to do with the rest of my life.

At night I couldn't sleep. I felt I was closing off all possibilities for myself. But I also felt guilty about Jean. We'd been sleeping together for almost a year, and I felt I owed her marriage if that was what she wanted. She'd seemed so offbeat and Bohemian at first. Now her parents were inviting me to dinner on the Grand Concourse. They were perfectly decent people, but I couldn't stand being with them.

I felt I was indebted to Jean, and the more I slept with her the more I was in debt, and then I needed more sex to stop thinking about it. I was trapped. I could have been a textbook case study of compulsive behavior. When we weren't having sex, we argued. Often Jean cried and told me I couldn't not get married. The invitations had been ordered. I told her my blood was being poisoned with cancer by my participation in the bourgeois act of marriage. I was paraphrasing Norman Mailer, whom I was reading at the time. But the invitations went out and the wedding loomed ahead.

A few days before the wedding I took a leave from Fort Dix. By then I could barely stand up. In desperation I called my brother, and told him how I felt and he said that I didn't have to get married. The family would still love me and stand behind me. I hadn't been close to my brother in years, but I felt as if he was saving me from drowning.

I called Jean to let her know I wasn't going through with it, and she started screaming over the phone and insisted I tell her parents in person. An hour later we drove to the Grand Concourse and sat down in her parents' living room. Jean stared at me with hatred. Her father tried to convince me to go through with it. "Just try it out," he said. "You can always separate if it doesn't work out." I kept repeating that I couldn't get married to anyone right then. I offered to pay whatever expenses they had incurred and to help Jean find a new place. My offers were angrily refused. Her father said he wanted to punch me in the nose. I told him I understood how he felt and left, with Jean sobbing on her mother's shoulders. For the next two weeks I hid in my room at my parents' apartment until I had to return to Fort Dix.

Three years later I ended up marrying Jean, still feeling guilty over the pain I had inflicted. Our marriage lasted eight years.

Over time I occasionally ran into Philip Roth on the street. The first time he nodded, but after that he didn't remember me. I, of course, recognized him. I saw his picture in newspapers and magazines and on book jackets all the time. I knew he'd had a tumultuous first marriage and that his wife had died in a car accident. Much later his marriage to the actress Claire Bloom ended acrimoniously. I read that he had a quadruple heart bypass and later suffered a nervous breakdown. Now he lived a reclusive but productive life in Connecticut.

Not long ago I saw him strolling toward me on Eighty-third Street and Amsterdam. He was wearing a short casual jacket and looked handsome and fit. By coincidence I had just finished reading his most recent book, *The Dying Animal*, which I had liked a lot. I had an impulse to say hello and re-introduce myself, but I knew that would be pretty ridiculous—Hi, Philip, I knew you forty years ago, I married the girl I introduced you to on Stuyvesant Street. It didn't work out. How have you been?

He had written all his books and received all his rewards but, like me, had taken some lumps along the way. He walked past me without a glance, and I stopped and turned and watched as he continued on.

Fort Dix

In the winter Fort Dix, New Jersey, was a dreary, cold, damp place; in the summer it was dreary, hot, and humid. I was there for two years, starting in January, 1959, and for the last twenty months as clerk of Company F, Second Training Regiment. Company clerk duty meant getting up at four-thirty or five and typing the morning report before the soldiers left on maneuvers, so Captain Green could sign it and I could take it to Battalion Headquarters, a few minutes walk away. Then I'd have breakfast in the mess hall with some of the cooks, who piled food on my plate. I sometimes typed official letters for them—requests for transfers or inquiries about pay. They appreciated my help and considered me intelligent. I did feel smart or at least literate next to the basic training cadre who hadn't been to college, though they were wise in the ways of the world. Anyway, I liked them all and was proud that they seemed to like me.

The sergeants acted demanding and tough in front of the recruits, but they were decent, fun-loving men. Sergeant Rooney played fiddle on weekends at square dances off base. Sergeant McGuane had been at Pearl Harbor and talked nostalgically about the Second World War and sang off-color songs with lines like, "Fuck, fuck, fuck it, Joe kicked the bucket." The company commander, Captain Green, was a dark-skinned, broad-shouldered black man who'd been promoted to officer on the battlefield during the Korean War.

Even 1st Sergeant Dzieniewski, who could go off the deep end sometimes, wasn't so bad. He was a thin, nervous man who worried about things going wrong, like the time the milk for the company had been delivered to the mess hall on a hot day and left to spoil outside until a major from Battalion Headquarters drove by and noticed it and chewed everyone out. But when everything was going smoothly Sergeant Dzieniewski was fair and even-tempered, the way most everyone else was. He and Captain Green appreciated my diligence as a clerk and sometimes praised me. Even though I hadn't been trained in an Army clerical school, I was well suited for my job. I was a fast typist and I was happy to be working hard for the first time in my life, and to have a feeling of accomplishment. I adopted the swagger of the sergeants, went out without a jacket during the winter cold as they did and, like Sergeant Dzieniewski, smoked Camels.

Basic training lasted eight weeks, then there'd be a break for a couple of days until a new group arrived. Usually a few recruits couldn't endure the pressure of training and would eventually be discharged as Section 8s, or psychos, supposedly prohibited forever from finding respectable employment. I remember Sergeant Dzieniewski screaming at a new recruit that he would personally tie the young man's pecker with a rubber band if he didn't stop wetting his bed. Another recruit from Great Neck, Long Island, stole hangers from the supply room and tried to sell them to the other recruits for a quarter each. There were other occasional minor disturbances—someone who didn't make it back from a weekend pass and ended up in the brig—but in general things went smoothly. Some of the training companies consisted of National Guardsmen in for six months instead of two years, and they were generally older and more mature. One group arrived after the New York State law board exams, and soon dozens of the new recruits received telegrams informing them they had passed. The sergeants joked that they had to be extra careful how they treated a fucking bunch of lawyers, or they might get sued.

One group of National Guardsmen included Nelson Rockefeller's son, Michael. Tall and wiry, with thick glasses, he was chosen as head of his platoon, and was very careful about the money he doled out for cleaning materials. At mess hall he ate slowly and chatted with the cooks, asking them why they were Democrats and not Republicans. He went about his training seriously, scoring high on physical training, but didn't do so well in marksmanship because of his weak eyesight. The few times he came into the orderly room he spoke seriously and respectfully and gave me the sense that he was a man who expected to live up to the achievements of his famous family. In our company Ping-Pong tournament he competed with flare, obviously an experienced player, but because he kept his boots on, he kept slipping and was eliminated by someone less skillful who played in bare feet and merely kept the ball in play.

I envied Rockefeller his sense of purpose and entitlement. In comparison, I was just putting in my time, up early to type the morning reports, then sitting around chewing the fat with the sergeants. A few evenings a week I would walk a couple of miles to the library to return books and take out new ones.

At the end of his basic training Rockefeller was assigned to the Army Intelligence School at Fort Devens, Massachusetts. He would be discharged in four months. I had another year left. While he was at Fort Devens he was stopped twice for speeding on the Mass Turnpike. The second time the case made the *New York Times* and Rockefeller was quoted as saying that he'd been doing eighty and the highway patrolman had been correct to stop him. I imagined him saying this to the reporter respectfully and with self-assurance. To Michael Rockefeller, I thought, everything must have seemed an adventure. My own life felt empty in comparison. My biggest achievement was being the best company clerk in the Second Training Regiment.

In January 1961, armed with a Certificate of Achievement from the Commanding General of Fort Dix, I found a job as an investigator for the New York City Department of Welfare. At my first day of orientation I saw Barry Malzberg, one of the recruits I had processed out on a Section 8, also beginning his training.

Soon after, the papers were filled with stories of Michael Rockefeller's disappearance while on an expedition in the South Pacific. He and an anthropologist were in a canoe that capsized off the south coast of Dutch New Guinea; the two of them kept afloat by holding onto the debris. Despite his companion's advice to wait for help, Rockefeller decided to try to swim ashore. The next morning the anthropologist was rescued, but Rockefeller was never found.

A year later I left the Welfare Department for a job at the New York City Youth Board as a street worker with gangs. I liked it better, though the pay was less. I was beginning to have hope that I would eventually flounder my way into something I actually enjoyed doing.

Central Park West

A few months after my discharge from the Army, I was still living at home. One afternoon I got off early from my Welfare Department job, took the subway downtown, and then started walking along Central Park West toward my parents' apartment. A friend had recently told me about a studio apartment in the East Village, but I wasn't sure if I wanted to move to that part of town. When I was nearly in front of my parents' building, a Con Ed worker jumped out of a ditch and yelled, "Hey, Schrader, it's me, Joe Gargano." He pointed me out to his fellow workers. "We were buddies in the Army," he told them. He was short and muscular and had a heavy New York accent. We'd been in basic training together in the middle of winter, and the first thing I remembered about him was that he'd stolen my gloves At the beginning of basic there'd been a rash of stolen gloves. I had just received a second pair from the supply sergeant and was about to stamp my serial number on them. But before I could we were ordered outside. When I returned, Gargano, whose cot was next to mine, was stamping a pair of gloves.

"Hey, my gloves are missing," I shouted.

"Gee, that's too bad," Gargano said, as he put the gloves into his foot locker. "You can't trust anyone around here."

It wasn't altogether surprising that I would be the victim of a theft. The first weekend in basic my father, without telling me that he was coming, had driven up to the orderly room in his chauffeured Cadillac to find out how I was doing . Everyone crowded around the car and word soon spread who it belonged to. I started playing the part of the modest rich kid who didn't lord his wealth over everyone. It was an easy part to play. I didn't have to do anything but be soft-spoken and humble.

"You live around here?" Gargano asked.

I pointed to my parents' building, with its canopy and ornate, wrought iron, black grill fence.

"Jesus, that's a fancy place."

"I manage," I said, still playing the part.

His co-workers called to him to get back to work. "Well, nice seeing you, Schrader."

We shook hands and said goodbye. When I got home, I called my friend to find out how soon I could look at that apartment in the East Village.

The Purple Dragons

In 1962, when I went to work for the New York City Youth Board, street gangs were still active. Drugs hadn't wiped them out yet, as they would in a few years. Youth workers hung out with gangs on the street, took them on trips, and referred them to programs that helped them find jobs. I was assigned to the Purple Dragons on East Fourth Street between Avenues B and C. Scrawled frequently on the building walls were the letters DLAMF, short for Down Like a Mother Fucker, which meant that the Dragons were ready for action at a moment's notice.

It took me a few months to discover that the Purple Dragons no longer existed. Primo, the acknowledged leader, was a legend on the Lower East Side. He was by then nineteen, had been visited and worked with by all the community agencies in the area, and was studied in depth by the New York University School of Social Work. He was short, with a thick neck and broad shoulders, and usually wore a small black fedora and smoked a cigar. The first time we met he did a few backward flips on the sidewalk and then wanted to wrestle with me, but I told him that was against the rules. "How come Julio used to wrestle with us?" he asked. Julio, the previous street worker, had been a nationally recognized athlete and hero in Puerto Rico.

"He was breaking the rules," I said. "He could have gotten fired."

Primo was a nonstop talker, and tried to impress me with stories of his adventures. He told me about the time he'd led his gang down to Henry Street to fight Tarzan, the leader of the Henry Street Dragons, one on one. When he saw how immense and muscular Tarzan was, Primo modified his challenge to an exchange of punches to the stomach.

Tarzan went first, and whacked Primo in the solar plexus. When Primo recovered, he did the same to Tarzan. Then they shook hands, and Primo returned to the storefront room where he lived on Fourth Street, went to bed for two days, and spat up blood. Later he and Tarzan became friends. By the time I met Tarzan he had retired from the streets and worked in the neighborhood as a dog groomer. He seemed like a sweet and gentle young man, though I still wouldn't have wanted to exchange punches in the stomach with him.

Another time Primo jumped about eight feet from the roof of one seven-story building to another one. He and about twenty other boys had been going up there for two weeks, trying to work up the courage to try it. "What did I have to lose, I finally figure?" Primo said. "If I make it I'm a hero. If I don't, fuck it, I'm dead. So I jump, and I make it. Then Flaco makes it, and Jackie, and Pollo, and six or seven other guys until Gordo tries, and has to hold on with his hands till we pull him up." When I met him, I realized that Gordo was a nickname meaning fat.

But now Primo's main activity seemed to be going to Brooklyn and Queens at night with a few friends to steal car parts, then selling them to auto repair shops. The only thing Primo was interested in doing with me was going to Coney Island, where I paid for rides, so one night I took him and three others there. They went right to the Cyclone. I was afraid of heights, so I sat where the tickets were sold and watched them get on: Primo and Jackie, the high school dropout with a one hundred and thirty-seven IQ, and the Rodriguez brothers, Eddie and Willie, thin and handsome boys of twenty and twenty-one who always had girls around them. As the ride finished each time, they screamed with pleasure and asked me to buy them another ride. Primo kept yelling at me from the front seat to get on with them. "Don't be a faggot, Jim," he shouted. He called most male adults Jim: policemen, social workers, clerks in stores.

Finally, by the third time, I got so angry at his taunts that I jumped onto the seat behind him. We chugged slowly up to the first and highest point of the ride. As we reached the top, the cars seemed to hesitate and then stop before beginning their downward surge. I could see all the way down to the lights of the concessions and to the apartment buildings beyond the amusement park. I felt as if our little car was going to fly off the tracks. Primo stood up and leaned out sideways and thrust one hand in the air, holding on with the other hand to the steel bar that was supposed to lock him into his seat. "I'm Primo!" he screamed to all of Coney Island and to the rest of Brooklyn as we shot down the tracks. I was sure I was going to die. "Sit down, Primo," I begged. "Please!" I closed my eyes and prayed to God to let me live through this. When the ride was over, I staggered off and fell onto the wooden bench at the entrance to the Cyclone. I refused to buy any more tickets, and soon we went home. "You're okay, Jim," Primo said to me on the subway, still laughing about the last ride.

The next day I met with my supervisor and was reassigned to the Third Street Dragons, a younger group on East Third Street between First and Second Avenues. That night I found Primo in a bar and bought him a farewell beer. He was already pretty drunk. "My father was a drunk," he said. "I'll end up a drunk, too."

I tried to argue with him, telling him how smart he was and how everybody respected him.

"I'm just a goddamn Spic, Jim," he said. He bit into his glass and broke a piece off the top. Then he spit bits of glass from his mouth, and wiped away blood from a cut on his tongue. He looked a little dazed at what he'd done. "I'm just a goddamn drunk, like my father." He put his head down on the bar and went to sleep.

The next night I introduced myself to the Third Street Dragons. They were fourteen and fifteen years old, and liked to hang out in front of the candy store near First Avenue and listen to doo-wop on the juke box. I could tell they were pleased to be considered important enough to have a street worker assigned to them. Compared to Primo, they looked very innocent.

Part IV　Mixed Feelings

Plugging In

In the summer of 1965 I attended a reading institute for teachers at Yeshiva University. For a year and a half I had been teaching English in a junior high school, where most of my students had reading problems. The professors at Yeshiva stressed the mechanics of reading, using cards and slides to diagnose a student's weaknesses—things like recognizing initial consonants and understanding vowel sounds. Then they used a different set of materials to correct these weaknesses. They called this plugging a student in.

I found the Yeshiva materials boring and sterile and wondered how helpful they really were. A number of my students had difficulties that seemed beyond these diagnostic solutions. Many of them were bright and articulate but had trouble concentrating and remembering. I felt they had individual complexities and variations in their thinking that couldn't be diagnosed as easily as my professors claimed. Yet I had no substitute theory to offer, and I participated in the course as best I could, even though I found it tedious and wished I was doing something that interested me more and that I believed in.

In the fall I went back to my school in the Bronx, using some of the approaches I had learned at Yeshiva, but not making any more headway than I had previously. To begin with, I didn't enjoy teaching. I had butterflies in my stomach each day as I drove up the West Side Highway and then onto the Cross Bronx Expressway to the west Bronx near Crotona Park where my school was located.

I needed thirty graduate credits to earn an increment in my salary. After struggling through some boring education courses, I discovered I could instead take creative writing for part of the requirement, and in the spring semester I enrolled in a class at City College. The professor was a sour, failed writer who had been working on a novel for years. As an undergraduate he'd been in a famous writing class at City along with Bernard Malamud, who had gotten a B. That was a high grade, my professor told the class, and implied that we wouldn't do as well. But I didn't care about grades; I could now concentrate on something that had meaning for me.

I began getting up at 5:30 every morning and writing in my notebook for half an hour or so. I described how mundane and unhappy my existence was and felt that somehow by doing this I would be able to make myself into someone special, to prove that I had intelligence and talent. I told how I lived in a dark four-room apartment on 87th Street between Columbus and Amsterdam Avenues with my wife and infant son, Daniel. Our windows looked onto the back of an apartment house on 86th Street and I grew familiar with some of my neighbors: a fat lady who lived alone with her two young children and often walked around in a slip and brassiere; a young couple who each night sat facing each other in opposite armchairs without speaking. I changed my son's smelly diapers every morning because my wife didn't like to get up early and was usually still sleeping when I left for work. Sometimes I woke up at three a.m. and felt the walls were closing in on me. Maybe because of my own unhappy childhood or my uneven academic record, I had no talent as a teacher. I didn't know many facts and wasn't analytical, so it was hard for me to explain things to students, despite my fondness for them. Mainly, I wanted to find out about their lives and talk with them about books. But they needed facts and discipline. My classes often became chaotic and I ended up giving impromptu spelling tests to quiet the kids down. I'd say a word out loud then use it in a sentence and ask them to spell it correctly on their test papers. Explosion, I'd say, the man put a gun to his head and then there was a loud explosion.

One morning at home when I sat down at my desk to write I remembered how the Yeshiva professors had talked about plugging kids into their reading materials. I imagined plugging into my own life, bypassing my brain and writing directly from my feelings. I pictured a thick, electrical cord running from my stomach to my notebook, and I started writing down words without thinking. I wrote more freely than ever before and had trouble stopping when I heard Daniel cry out from his crib. Every morning after that I imagined plugging in and was able to start writing immediately. Sometimes I even got up an hour earlier.

Each week I'd bring what I had written to class and the professor would read it out loud. He had many criticisms but he sometimes conceded that I had a certain flair. The next semester I found a more congenial course in Columbia University's General Studies program and within two years I quit teaching to become a full-time student in writing at the Columbia School of the Arts. When I finished my MFA my wife and I divorced. I found an administrative job at Teachers and Writers Collaborative, an arts education group that sent writers into schools. It was the first job I had ever actually liked. Somewhere along the way I lost the habit of plugging in and could manage to write only sporadically. But still l felt more fulfilled and hopeful than before and sometimes I remembered the reading course at Yeshiva nostalgically. It had helped change my life in a way I couldn't have predicted.

The Canoe

In 1969 Jean and I bought a house on Fire Island, where we spent only two summers before separating. At the end of each summer vacation there Jean would return depressed. She said she hated the drabness of the city and dreaded the oncoming winter.

Our last summer together Jean was always unhappy, and I felt it was my fault. I brought her flowers and gifts when I came out weekends, but nothing seemed to lighten her spirits. When she insisted she wanted a canoe, I tried to argue her out of it. What would we do with one? I asked. It would be difficult to carry down to the shore, and the ocean was usually too rough to paddle in anyway. But I gave in and we drove to a Sears Roebuck, bought an aluminum canoe, and tied it on top of our car.

We hardly used the canoe. Sometimes neighbors borrowed it, but otherwise it sat in our shed. At the end of August my cousin Phil and his new wife Naomi came out for the weekend. They both loved outdoor sports and their eyes lit up when they saw the canoe. It was a sunny day and the waves were mild, and I watched them paddle far out, the crests of the waves periodically hiding the canoe. I could hear their laughter, and I felt envious of their high spirits and energy and their joy in being together.

That winter Jean and I separated. She got to keep the house and, along with it, the canoe, but as far as I know she never used it.

The following May, Phil and Naomi had a son. When I visited them Phil told me that he had been conceived that afternoon in the canoe. I started laughing for what seemed like the first time in months. At least the damn thing had served some useful purpose.

The Icing on the Cake

In August at our beach house, a few months before Jean and I separated, she baked a chocolate cake and set it on the kitchen table to cool. "Tell Daniel not to touch it," she said in that angry way we had taken to speaking to each other that summer. "I'm going for a swim."

Our son Daniel was nearly six, a big precocious boy who was used to getting his own way. I was reading in the living room, annoyed with Jean for leaving the house so abruptly and assigning me to police her cake. I told Daniel to stay away from it and continued reading. When Jean returned she discovered Daniel's fingerprints all over the icing and began yelling. "You know what you can do with your fucking cake," I answered, and ended up driving back to the city by myself.

By November we had agreed to a separation, and one afternoon I sat on the sofa with Daniel and told him his mother and I were getting a divorce. "We love you very much," I explained in a way I thought would ease his pain, "but your mother and I aren't able to get along."

Daniel began crying and crawled onto my lap. "Tell Mom it was my fault," he sobbed. "You told me not to touch the cake."

I put my arms around him and hugged him. "It wasn't the cake. We just don't get along."

"Tell Mom I'm sorry," Daniel said between sobs, and ran to his room.

First Days of Divorce

I was angry at Jean for sending Daniel to a Rudolph Steiner school. They were fascistic, culture-minded, humorless, mystical phonies. I visited with him at Open House a few days after my divorce came through, and I had agreed to pay for the school.

I got pulled into a lecture given by the headmaster. A big, flamboyant, bullshit artist. Openness, wholeness, unity. The audience looked like vegetarians, faddists. A man across the aisle wore a black sport jacket, a huge velvet bow tie, shiny leather boots. People took notes. Openness, wholeness, unity. Old ladies nodded. The parents seemed so pleased with themselves and with Steiner.

It was 19th century mysticism. A Dostoyevsky novel. A parody. I didn't see a face I liked in the audience of seventy-five. Maybe I was a bit mad myself.

I went up to the classroom afterward. It was small and bare. Plants in the window. Children's paintings on the wall, but the room was small and depressing. I never should have come.

The teacher greeted me. She was a thin, beautiful woman, ethereal-looking. She looked like a nurse or a nun. I sensed hospital and sickness from her.

"I'm sorry you had to sit through the lecture," she said. "I could see you squirming. I know you don't believe in this, aren't ready."

I hadn't realized she was behind me at the lecture. Maybe I would have tried to be more still, out of politeness.

"I've been meaning to talk to you about your son," she said. "He's not happy here. It may be too late. He's been contaminated by public school."

She told me he was disruptive. That he'd changed the class. She'd had most of the children since the first grade. It was now the fifth, and she'd have them till the eighth. She needed support from the parents. I let him watch television and he wasn't supposed to, she said. I was dumbfounded and furious. He was a wonderful child. Brilliant, energetic, creative, loving. But I wondered. He was aggressive. Wanted to shine. Grabbed things, pushed kids. He needed to learn not to.

"They're little buds that we're helping to make grow," she said. "We fill them with our model. Next week we start zoology and we teach mutuality. We don't want parents talking about Darwin and survival of the fittest and upsetting our ideas. You have to be supportive."

My head was reeling. I didn't even know what mutuality was. I supposed it was some kind of love between species, between all creatures.

"He's my son," I said. "He's only ten years old. You people are nuts." I pointed to the paintings on the walls. "Why does everything look like a rainbow?"

It was true. All yellow and pink and green. Big fluffy rainbow fields.

"We give them models here for truth and beauty and self-control," she said.

Parents wandered in. Daniel ran into the room and out with another child. The teacher said she'd talk to my ex-wife and then to me again.

I walked down the stairs. At the next floor Steiner's books were on display for sale. I leafed through them. They were written in abstractions, not English. I couldn't bear to buy one and have to hold it in my hand. I put it down. The lady at the desk was wearing a dress with a full skirt and had that ethereal look. They all did.

There were displays of children's crafts on the first floor. Woodworking and knitting and art. Everything was serene. I was in a loony bin of beauty and truth and culture.

I walked out into the street with Daniel. I gave him a squeeze. He ran down the block to let off steam.

That night after I'd taken him back to his mother, looking for a parking spot, I turned off Riverside Drive and saw a space just up the block in front of my building at 114th Street. I waited for the car behind to go past me before I backed in, but instead he pulled into the spot. I was furious, but there was nothing I could do. It took me a long time to find another space. When I finally reached my building I picked up a thick pebble at the curb and walked around the car that had taken my spot, scratching off the finish in a scraggly line.

Single Again

Women began to obsess me. I had lost my confidence after the divorce, even though I could rationalize by saying Jean was deeply depressed. I was thirty-eight, but I felt like an old man, past my prime.

I was still working at Teachers and Writers Collaborative, and I took out a friend of one of the artists. Anne was twenty-five, tall and beautiful, and had just broken up with her boyfriend. When we were in bed, she told me he was much taller than me and she missed him and wasn't ready to start a relationship with anyone else.

I answered a personal ad in the *New York Review of Books* by a woman who was a short story writer. We met for drinks in the Village and argued about short stories. She was an attractive blonde with glasses who had a religious, conservative bent and believed you needed an outline before you wrote anything. I argued for instinct and improvisation. I was sure we also disagreed on everything else. We coldly shook hands at the subway entrance.

I pursued a woman who was active on my block committee and offered to help her distribute the block paper, but she told me that she already had enough help. I watched from my window as she walked from building to building, carrying copies of the paper, alongside a handsome young journalist who lived nearby.

I wrote a number of stories about women and men in unsatisfying, unloving relationships. When the man wanted the woman, she wasn't available, and when the woman wanted the man, he wasn't ready. In one story a woman puts a collar around a man's neck and leads him around like a dog and both keep tugging at the leash. After a while this turns them both on. In another story a writer goes out with his editor and writes articles about everything they do, like taking baths together. His articles are a great success, but they break up, which he also writes an article about. In another, someone rents a studio apartment from his friend's girlfriend, who has moved in with his friend. The girlfriend still feels attached to the place and likes to spend time there, and he allows her to, in exchange for sex.

And all the time I kept going out. There was Sherry, an artist who was a lot like my ex-wife—bright and offbeat, but not too stable. Then came Lynne, a large blonde schoolteacher who worked hard and unsuccessfully at achieving an orgasm. After that came Sally, the ex-girlfriend of an old friend of mine, which made me feel a little incestuous and, though she was nice, I stopped calling. There were a couple of others I can't quite remember, and then there was another schoolteacher, Sylvia, who had a terrific body but was insecure and felt that men liked her for her body. (I kept thinking my father would be proud of me for dating a knockout like Sylvia.) She was from California and had never tried to adopt a New York manner, which made her seem a little slow, even though she wasn't.

But I didn't worry about the feelings of the women I dated. I was just trying to work out my own life. Once I succeeded in sleeping with someone, I got an instinctive guilty feeling that I should marry her or go out with her exclusively. But this feeling disappeared right away because I had just ended a marriage. I had to sleep with x amount of women before I regained my self-respect and avenged myself on Jean, who had initiated the divorce or at least instigated it by refusing to sleep with me. Near the end of our marriage, I had discovered that she was in love with someone else. I found a letter from him hidden in her drawer and xeroxed it for my lawyer. I still can't believe the depth of emotion I felt when I found it. My hands trembled at the copy shop. My lawyer scoffed at the letter. All it said was that he'd kissed her once in a phone booth.

So I caused unpleasant breakups. I didn't call back after a weekend with someone. Or I'd be sullen and un-talkative at breakfast the next morning. I was critical of women, the way my father was of my mother. He hardly ever said a pleasant word to her, and she had grown more and more depressed over the years. Or maybe she first became depressed and then he became unpleasant. My father bullied women, and I unconsciously tried to imitate him and dominate girlfriends as he had my mother.

Yet at the same time I wanted to save women, the way I had hoped to save my mother, somehow make her happy, an attempt doomed to fail, of course. No one can make anyone else happy. Not my mother, anyway. Her depression was as deep and permanent and unalterable as waves in the ocean.

So I was a mass of guilt—guilt about sex, guilt about not being a savior—and at the same time wanting to screw 'em and leave 'em. I was seeing a therapist, but he mostly talked about his woodworking and silversmithing, and how soothing hobbies could be.

On Saturdays I took Daniel to play tennis in Connecticut, which also meant a pleasant drive and then lunch nearby before driving home. During his lesson I would play on another court. One of my regular partners was a retired advertising man. While we were taking a shower one day, he offered to fix me up with his neighbor Sandra, who was separated from her husband.

Sandra drove into the city to meet me for dinner. We ate at an East Side restaurant and finished a bottle of wine. Sandra was a tall, slender brunette with an easy, knowing laugh. She was different from the women I was used to, well-groomed in a suburban manner, hair set at a beauty parlor, eye shadow, cashmere sweater, and knit skirt. She talked in a sophisticated, cynical way, a little like someone out of an Updike novel, and smoked and drank a lot. There was something WASP-ish about her, even though her parents were Polish Roman Catholics.

I started driving up to Stamford, Connecticut, where she lived in a house near the water. The first few times I got lost and kept calling to ask directions, until Sandra gave me the ultimatum to either follow her instructions or not bother to come at all. She could be a little frightening and intimidating. After that I learned to get there on my own. She told me about her ex-husband, whom she called weak and unambitious, and whom she had stopped loving a long time before the end of their marriage. She had had a number of affairs, the most serious with a young priest who later dropped out of the priesthood. After her divorce, she had gone out with Jack, a successful businessman who cheated on her. "He was Jewish like you," Sandra said. "But more aggressive. He was a handsome son of a bitch. I still miss him."

Sandra's nine-year-old son had behavior problems in school. Sometimes she used him as an excuse not to see me. Her excuses came late and seemed a little hazy, but nothing stopped me. I was intrigued by the suburbs.

Sandra took me to a party where I met the mayor of Stamford. He drank a lot and gave me the feeling that he was not above corruption and dealmaking. At the party everyone gossiped about who was sleeping with whom. I felt more like a country bumpkin than a city slicker from New York. But sometimes Sandra and I had idyllic evenings. She was a good cook and prepared romantic candlelight meals, which we ate on her porch overlooking Long Island Sound.

I never knew what mood she'd be in. Sometimes she was warmly affectionate and other times angry and sullen. She often had headaches and took pills prescribed by her doctor. We drank a lot, much more than I was accustomed to—martinis or Scotch before dinner, and wine during and after. I started smoking again, just to keep her company, though without inhaling since I'd never learned how.

At the time I first met Sandra, I'd been seeing Sylvia, the knockout schoolteacher, but I'd dropped her without an explanation. In our last phone conversation, Sylvia told me that she'd cried in front of her third-grade class after I'd broken our final date. I never bothered to apologize or tried to explain why. How could I? I didn't know why myself. And yet all the time I thought of myself as a nice guy, just a little confused.

Sandra knew how to keep my interest. She kept me guessing and was critical of me, like a demanding parent. She told me I looked like a cab driver with my short, zip-up jackets. Sometimes I went away ecstatic, other times devastated. We talked of going to Vermont on Memorial Day weekend, but a few days before she called and said she couldn't go. "I've gotten back with Jack," she said. "I've been seeing him for a while."

Maybe she'd never stopped seeing him, I thought. I mumbled a few words and said goodbye. I scheduled an extra session with my therapist. He told me to try and learn from my experience, the way he did after he ruined a piece of wood when he was woodworking.

I knew I had to change how I was living. I had the feeling it would take a long time. Maybe the rest of my life.

My Father's Shadow

Every time I visited my father after I became director of Teachers and Writers Collaborative, he would ask me what it was exactly that I did for a living. I would patiently explain to him that T&W sent writers into schools and published a magazine and books about their work and that I was the director. My job was to supervise the program and raise the funds to support it. I didn't make much money, I explained, but I was proud of what we did. My father never remembered, even when I wrote it down for him. I think the concept was beyond him. Why would anyone choose to work for a nonprofit organization when capitalism offered one the opportunity to make as much money as one could?

Near the end of my first year at the job, I managed to secure a large grant from a private foundation. When I told my father about it, he asked, "Do they know that I'm your father?"

"I don't think so," I said. "We got it for the work we do in schools." But for the rest of the day I walked around feeling dizzy. Perhaps one of the officers in the foundation had heard of my father and somehow that knowledge had helped.

No matter what I did in life, I couldn't seem to escape my father's shadow.

Mixed Feelings

At the time I met my second wife, Alice, I had two cats. That was nearly twenty-five years ago, and I don't remember their names, but I do remember that I enjoyed them very much. One was given to me by Daniel soon after the divorce, and the other by a poet friend, Laura, who cleaned my house once a week. Laura believed that a writer should do something connected to reality and not just live in isolation. Later she became a pediatric nurse at Sloan-Kettering, and still later moved to San Francisco. One day she found a tiny kitten in the street and took it home, but her dog wouldn't accept it, so she brought it to my house when she came to clean. The kitten had been traumatized in the street and hid under the refrigerator the first few weeks, but finally came out and soon was playing with my other cat.

By the time I started going out with Alice, the cats had bonded, and they played and leaped around the house. To be honest, I wasn't an experienced or conscientious cat owner, and they shed hair all over the furniture and clothing, and the litter box smelled. Alice was orderly and didn't like animals to begin with so, as a condition of her moving in, she insisted I give them away. This was difficult for me because, despite their wildness, I liked them and also because my son was very fond of them. He stayed with me one day a week and every other weekend, and he considered the cats part of our family.

But finally I did give them away to my friends Bill and Annie, artists who lived in a large loft in Chinatown. A year later they had to have the cats put away because they started biting people as well as each other. The vet thought they had developed brain tumors, which Bill and Annie speculated might have come from the paint fumes in the loft.

Alice always jokes that I had a hard time choosing between her and the cats, whereas I still resent that she wasn't able to adjust to them. If she had been, they would probably have lived a lot longer.

Diane

A few weeks before I was to marry Alice I developed a crush on Diane, a girl in the office twenty years younger than I. I was once again working for my father and brother in the dress business, hoping I would be able to prove myself to them this time, and also thinking it would be my last chance to make a large amount of money.

Diane was a receptionist in her mid-twenties, and I sat about fifty feet from her. One day I looked up from my desk and noticed for the first time how thin her waist was and how graceful her movements were. She had wide shoulders and full breasts, but she also seemed very delicate. Her hair was light brown and lustrous, and her skin was smooth and healthy looking. She always looked as if she'd just had a glass of milk.

Of course I didn't say anything to her, because I knew we had nothing in common. I had seen pictures of her boyfriend, a big strapping fellow wearing the soccer uniform of the club he played for on Sundays. She had a large group of friends on Long Island of Irish and Italian and German descent. They did things like go to parades for the Islanders after they'd won the hockey championship. Once she'd missed a day's work because she'd pulled a muscle dancing at a friend's wedding.

I hardly talked to her, though I loved to hear her boyish, deep voice and Long Island accent that dropped final g's. She said commonplace, ordinary things, but I strained to hear them, happy that her looks hadn't made her standoffish and arrogant, though a little surprised that her beauty didn't house a brilliant mind.

I had no idea what she thought of me. Most likely she didn't think of me at all. I was just someone she paged for phone calls. Still, I tried to detect some response on her part, tried to impart my admiration of her, silently, through the air so it might be reciprocated.

The closer my wedding came, the more desperately I fantasized. I wondered what was wrong with me. Was it the pressure of getting married again? Or the big wedding Alice and her family had arranged?

Or had I not waited long enough for the right woman, who had then appeared too late? Because it was too late. I was going to get married. I was going to move into a co-op and I was going to have more children. That was final. I had agreed, so had Alice, and she wasn't the type to back out.

The Friday before the wedding was rainy and overcast, a dreamy strange day on which it didn't feel right going to work. The subway was delayed and I came in late. Diane rode up in the elevator with me.

"Did you have trouble coming in?" I asked.

"Yes," she said, more quickly and easily than she usually responded. "There was mist on the bridge when we started, and the train crawled for miles."

She looked at me as if to reinforce just how unusual the scene had been, how the train seemed to float in space forever. I think it was the first time our eyes had met. Hers were an unusual bluish grey, cat's eyes. For the rest of the day I pictured her floating on a train in mist and fog, her beautiful eyes marveling at the strangeness.

The next week I left on a honeymoon to Italy. Friends drove us all over Rome and through mountain towns to the coast. The weather was sunny and clear and the food wonderful.

When I returned to work I felt guilty as I greeted Diane. I had hardly thought about her for weeks. I felt guilty for the secret thoughts I'd had about her before my marriage and guilty for having married someone else.

Soon after, my department was reorganized and my desk was changed, and I was no longer able to look at her all day.

A few years after that I decided to leave my job. Diane was still there, at the old place, in charge of all the clerical work, rarely working the switchboard anymore. She still saw the same boyfriend, or so I gathered from her friends at the office, but for some reason she wasn't planning to get married. She'd become a trifle older-looking, a little heavier at the waist and hips, but she was still extraordinarily beautiful, perhaps more beautiful than before.

After the small party they'd given me on my last day, when I said goodbye to her I wondered how someone so beautiful could do something like clerical work. But she seemed to like it, to need such an ordinary life. She wished me luck and smiled a beautiful smile.

The Need for a Watch

I often lose my watch because I take it off and put it on my lap and then forget about it. I don't like the feeling of a strap on my wrist, particularly when I am sitting still. So I don't allow myself to become upset when my watch disappears; I just buy another ten-dollar one. I usually wait a week or so because sometimes the watch turns up in a jacket or under a sofa cushion.

I didn't wear a watch until about ten years ago when I befriended Abdou, a Senegalese gypsy cab driver who used to drive my daughter and me to her school every morning and then bring me home again. At Christmas he gave my daughter Amelia a doll and me an imitation Cartier watch, like the ones the Senegalese vendors sell on the street for twenty or thirty dollars. Until then I always kept time in my head and could usually guess the approximate time without looking at a clock. Not wearing a watch gave me the illusion of being free from the constrictions of society. I felt I lived according to my own timetable, which, though it wasn't really true, pleased me when I thought about it.

Abdou had come to America to make money for his two families in Senegal, which totaled two wives and seven children. He was a gentle, seemingly simple soul who never really caught on to the rhythm of New York. I think I was his only customer. Sometimes I'd see him sitting perfectly still at the wheel as he waited for me. I wondered what was going on in his head. Was he saying a Muslim prayer or was his mind empty as he stared straight ahead? He reminded me of a deer in the woods, perfectly still, listening to the sounds around it. Sometimes I bought him a whole roasted chicken when I stopped to buy dinner on the way home in the morning. I felt guilty at having so much food. He always thanked me profusely, and would tell me the next day how he had shared it with the six or so other Senegalese drivers with whom he lived in East Harlem.

Once he went back to Senegal for a week because one of his daughters, who was the same age as mine, had died. His English wasn't very fluent, so I never found out the exact cause. He came back for another year, but then his visa expired, and this time when he left he couldn't return. Eventually the watch he'd given me broke, and I replaced it, since I could no longer tell time in my head. The need for a watch irritates me now, but wearing one also reminds me of my friendship with Abdou.

Luigi

"There's a new boy in class," Amelia said at dinner. "He's very funny. He bends over like this." Amelia bent over stiff-backed like an old man. "Then Stephanie pinches him," she said, "and he jumps in the air and yells ouch, like this. And then they do it again," she said, and she repeated her performance. Alice and I laughed.

"What's his name?" I asked.

"Luigi. He's from Brazil. He speaks Portuguese."

I imagined a short, stocky, dark-complexioned little boy with black hair.

"He doesn't know English except for a few words," Amelia said. "Sometimes he says goodbye and waves his arm and walks away and then he turns around and comes back and says hello." Amelia imitated him a few times, saying hello and goodbye in an accent that was meant to sound like Luigi.

"Is he learning to speak English?" I asked.

"A little."

"I bet he'll be speaking in a few months," I said.

"Oh, he'll be American by spring," Amelia said. "Yes, he'll be American by then."

Part V   My Father's Shoes

Job Interview

Mildred, the old housekeeper, was leaving to take care of her husband, who had become ill. She would still come in once a week to iron my father's shirts, but her departure would be a blow to my mother. Mildred was the only person my mother spoke to regularly, since by this time she and my father had little to do with one another. Mildred knew how to soothe her and lessen her depression. She was my mother's best friend.

My father asked me to bring the maid he had just interviewed in his office in midtown to meet my mother. Josephine was an elderly black woman, neatly dressed, with straightened hair. She was obviously respectable and intelligent, and my father seemed to like her. I accompanied her to the street and we rode uptown in my father's car to my parents' apartment on Central Park West. I tried to prepare her for the meeting.

"My mother can be difficult," I said. "She likes things her way, and sometimes her way can be a little strange."

"Well, I just try and do my job," Josephine said. "I've been doing this for forty years."

"Can I ask how old you are? It might come up when my mother meets you."

"I'm seventy."

I was surprised, since she looked at least fifteen years younger. "Perhaps I can give you some advice. My mother thinks she needs someone in her fifties or younger, even though the woman who has been working for her is around your age. It would be better if you told her you were sixty or so. You look much younger, anyway."

"I can't do that," Josephine said. "My church doesn't let me lie."

The employment agency had sent a younger woman to be interviewed the week before, but she had decided not to take the job, probably sensing how demanding my mother was. Now here was a dignified, intelligent woman who seemed to have the patience and understanding to care for my mother, but who didn't meet my mother's age requirements. My mother thought the supply of candidates was endless, and she was prepared to hold out until she found the perfect maid.

My mother was waiting with Mildred in the foyer when we arrived. She was in her best housecoat, bursting with energy and excitement. The apartment was the one area where she possessed power. My mother led Josephine into the kitchen and showed her the appliances and the pots and dishes.

"I like cleanliness," my mother said. She looked Josephine over as though Josephine were a horse, appraising her strength. "How old are you?"

"I'm seventy, Ma'am."

My mother walked to the pantry and asked Josephine to climb a small ladder and hand her a dish from the top shelf. Josephine did and my mother asked her to get another dish from the shelf.

"Mother, that's enough," I said.

"But I have to know how strong she is," my mother said to me.

I wanted to explain to Josephine that my mother wasn't always as awful as she seemed, but that sometimes she didn't understand what she was doing. At the end of the interview my mother told Josephine that she would speak to my father and come to a decision. I was certain that she had already dismissed her as a possibility because of her age. I left with Josephine. "I'm sorry about how my mother acted."

"I don't take it personally," Josephine said.

Later in the afternoon the employment agency called to complain about the treatment Josephine had received, and told my father they had no one left to apply for the position. The next day I tried to explain to my mother how insensitive and cruel she had been, and that she was going to end up stuck without anyone, but she just shook her head and said she knew what she needed.

Eventually my mother found a Haitian woman through another family in the building and, surprisingly, she worked out, even though she spoke little English. She was in her early forties, had a sweet disposition, and nodded in agreement at everything my mother said.

Chauffeurs

Passing the driving exam on his third try by slipping a twenty dollar bill onto the seat next to the examiner didn't make my father a good driver. He was stopped frequently by the police for infractions. Maybe at forty-six he was too old to learn or perhaps he didn't have the aptitude to begin with. So to drive his first car, a Lincoln Continental, which had elegant silver push buttons on the doors instead of handles, he hired Jimmy, the son of the assistant superintendent of our building in Washington Heights, whose family lived in a cold, dank apartment in the basement.

Jimmy was just beginning college at Hunter in the evening and was a gentle, bright young man, though he was bitter at how he'd been treated at P.S. 187, which was directly across the street from where we lived on Fort Washington Avenue. In the second grade, Miss Roberts, the principal, told him that he would be happier with his own people and transferred him to a school further downtown, in Harlem.

Jimmy wore a black cap and uniform and looked dignified. We were the only family in the neighborhood with a car and driver, and it set us apart. Having a chauffeur was the equivalent for me of wearing a sign that said, My father is richer than your father. I felt like a marked man, but in some ways I liked it. I knew people noticed, but I never mentioned having a chauffeur and tried, humbly, to appear like a normal person, even though I thought of myself as being a little like royalty. I'm sure this was the beginning of my inflated view of my father's wealth and power and, indirectly, my own. My father had done well in his world but, as I found out much later, he hadn't created the Rockefeller-like dynasty I imagined. After arriving from Poland at twenty-one, he started out in the garment industry as a deliveryman and then became a cutter, which was considered a good, secure job, but he wanted to run his own business and be his own boss. Later, after his success as a dress contractor, he took another gamble and became a manufacturer, designing and selling dresses directly to stores. Most of his money was invested in his own business, which supported many of his expenses. Other people with a similar income were more cautious and low-key in their spending, but my father took pleasure in going to nightclubs and racetracks and wearing custom-made clothing. He always felt he could earn still more, which he did.

In 1949, when we moved downtown to the larger apartment, Jimmy was replaced by Charles, a professional chauffeur, and the Lincoln by a large Cadillac with jump seats. Charles drove my father to work in the morning, then he came back for my mother to take her shopping or to a medical appointment. Sometimes my mother seemed hard pressed to think of activities to use him for. Within a few years she stopped using him altogether.

Charles grew bored with us; the next chauffeur was Booker, who worked as a shipping clerk for my father. Using him as a driver made financial sense, since he was already on the payroll. When he wasn't busy driving he could always pack boxes. The car became more and more a business tool. Booker shuttled buyers around during the day, and at night took my father to restaurants where he entertained department heads and store presidents. Booker was a round, lively man with a quick wit and a twinkle that everybody loved, and with his sociability was a good match for my father. Like him, Booker found girlfriends wherever he went, and he used the car for late night trysts after he took my father home. Several times my father found ladies' undergarments in the back seat and threatened to fire Booker, but they always made up. Booker worked twelve years, until he grew ill with diabetes. First he lost a leg and then went blind. He moved back home with relatives in Georgia and would call occasionally and speak to people at work. He was confined to sitting at home in a chair, he told them, but he was still dangerous if a woman came close to him.

His replacement was Ponce, a stocky, quiet man who, like Booker, worked in the shipping department. Unfortunately, Ponce had a drinking problem and, after several binges when he disappeared for a week or so, my father let him go. Reggie, the next chauffeur, was a professional with many excellent references. He was a competent driver, but he moonlighted after work, using the car to pick up passengers for extra cash. My father discovered this when he found a credit card in the back seat that someone had misplaced during an after-hours ride.

The last chauffeur was Joaquim, who worked for about thirteen years, until my father's death. My father had retired from the dress business and now went down to Wall Street every day to trade his own portfolio, so he got rid of his large Cadillac and switched to a smaller one. Joaquim, who was from Portugal, was well-educated and, despite his limited English, was able to discuss history and current events with my father as they drove around the city.

My father was not an easy man to work for. He always had to be right and could be critical and impatient, second-guessing things like the choice of avenues when traffic was heavy, but he was at his best with Joaquim, who became a close companion and friend to him. When Joaquim's daughter started college, my father paid part of her tuition. As he grew older, my father relied increasingly on Joaquim to help him in and out of the car and up stairs, and Joaquim was able to do this in a way that let my father retain his dignity and sense of independence. Joaquim enabled him to lead an active, vigorous life well into his nineties. My father's last chauffeur was his best.

My Father's Shoes

My father owned many custom-made suits and shirts, all carefully stored in closets and drawers, as well as a large supply of expensive silk undershorts, made by a company that had been out of business for many years by the time he died. But what impressed me the most were his shoes. He had nearly a dozen specially made pairs, all with shoe trees inside, wrapped in plaid woolen covers that resembled huge socks. He claimed that his feet were hard to fit, and that it took a long time to wear a pair in.

Mostly he wore black patent leather shoes, which he kept brightly polished and wore to work, though he also had sportier styles for the racetrack and vacations. The last ten years of his life, when he was going down to Wall Street, he stopped every morning in the lobby where he worked and had his shoes shined. He knew what pleased him.

I was walking with him in the street one day when he complained that the shoes he was wearing were beginning to crack and couldn't be repaired because the bootmaker who'd made them wasn't around anymore. My father at this time was in his early nineties.

"When did you buy them?" I asked.

"Oh, about fifty years ago."

I tried to tell him that he'd gotten pretty good wear out of them, but he wouldn't listen. He was irritated that his shoes were wearing out and that he'd have to break in another pair.

My Father's 75th Birthday Party

My father's 75th birthday party was held in a private room on the second floor of the restaurant La Grenouille. I brought the woman I was dating at the time, a college professor who dressed simply and wore little makeup. I had bought a suit for the occasion; when I walked into the room one of the waiters, noticing a tag on the sleeve of my jacket, stopped me politely and slipped it off the button it was attached to. "I got it for the party," I told him, embarrassed.

I had a few Scotches before dinner and then several glasses of wine with the meal. I was merely following my father's instructions. "You should always have a couple of drinks when you're with people," he used to tell me. "You're a lot more lively when you do." It was true. I felt lively, but I also felt dizzy.

My father's lawyer, Charlie Ballon, a tall, confident man who had played basketball at Columbia many years before, had arranged the party. The president of the Ladies Garment Workers' Union was also there. My mother, who by then had lost most of her ability to function socially, sat next to my girlfriend and kept telling stories about her childhood.

When the birthday cake was served, the speeches began. The union president, a long-winded, self-satisfied man, told how tough but fair my father was in bargaining with the union and how he understood workers because he had originally been a cutter. Charlie Ballon praised my father for his generous gifts to charitable causes and for his helpful participation in industry-wide efforts at improvement. Even my brother, who didn't enjoy speaking in public, told a funny story about my father that made him seem tough but loveable.

I hadn't realized that I was expected to speak, even after the cake was brought in and the speeches had begun, so I had nothing prepared. But that didn't prevent me from standing up just as the others had. I raised my glass of champagne. "To my father, Abe Schrader," I said, and waited for inspiration, but none came. "Here's to my father, Abe Schrader," I kept repeating loudly and drunkenly, hoping I was somehow expressing my love for him. My father looked at me with exasperation. "Enough already," he said. "We all know who your father is. Sit down."

The next morning when I woke up I remembered what a fool I'd made of myself. I began thinking of things I might have said, like when I was a boy and my father had taken me shopping for winter clothing and seemed to buy everything in the store, or the time we went to three separate movies on Broadway during the snowstorm of 1947 and then had dinner at the Sherry Netherland Hotel. Before I finished breakfast I had a warm, moving speech outlined in my head.

In Poland With My Father

In 1987 I took a trip to Poland with my father to visit his hometown of Ostralecko, two hours north of Warsaw. I first wrote about it a year or so later. A large section of that piece was about Tomek and Julita, a couple I met in Warsaw who, though living under repressive Communist rule, managed to survive in an interesting, offbeat way that I found appealing.

Around fifteen years later I went back to our trip to Poland, this time writing just about my father and me. My father had died two years before and I was still trying to come to terms with my memories of him. This second piece covers much of the same ground as the first, but with a somewhat different tone.

Tomek and Julita

My father hired Jerzy, a friendly, intelligent Polish man, to take us around, and Jerzy said he knew of a few luggage stores where my father might find a leather suitcase to replace the one that had got broken on the plane. "Remember, though, it's Poland," Jerzy said. "If you want umbrella, buy suitcase."

My father's leg bothered him and he wasn't able to walk much, so after a quick drive around Warsaw without finding a suitcase, he'd gone back to the hotel room. Jerzy drove me to a section called the old town and I bought some jewelry for my wife, a bright, folksy Cracow vest and skirt for my daughter, and some postcards. Warsaw had been almost completely destroyed by the Germans in the Second World War and the old town hadn't been rebuilt. Instead, on nearly every block were photos of how elegant and beautiful the area had looked before the devastation. Jerzy wanted to take me to Chopin's birthplace forty-five minutes outside of town, but we settled on the Wilanow Palace where Napoleon had slept, a beautiful castle with spacious gardens. Groups of sweet-looking children were shepherded around by their teacher and I examined them more closely than the gardens. I just wanted to meet Poles and walk around, but I was afraid of insulting Jerzy, who wanted to give me a tourist's view of Warsaw. A lively, friendly fellow, he spoke freely about how hard it was to live in Poland—the lines for food, the housing shortage—all with a fatalistic, comic tone. He made a lot of money for a Pole, but there wasn't much he could spend it on.

"I bought boat," he told me. "Sailboat with motor. My son want to take boat into water, but don't have time. I work for Japanese and they have me for next two months. My son not understand."

The Japanese, he told me, were okay to work for. "Pay is good, but they not talk. Busy with work, be on time, wait. No jokes. I pick up Japanese food for them in Frankfort every couple of months. Good pay, but boat not in water. Son disappointed."

On the way back to the hotel I noticed lines outside food stores. People standing patiently, talking to one another, looking at the sky, glancing at us as we passed by in the big Volvo, waiting, the way Jerzy waited for the Japanese.

At the hotel my father was putting a call through to his broker. He had arranged for the broker to send a telex at the end of every day so he'd know how his stocks were doing. There was a six-hour time difference, so now, late in the afternoon in Warsaw, the market was just opening in New York.

"Harry, my boy," my father said on the phone. "How'm I doing?"

I closed the door to the room my father was in and lay down on the bed and read until my eyes closed. When I woke I went into the other room, where my father was watching television. On the screen a man in a tie was reading the news in Polish.

The hotel had several restaurants and we went to the fanciest one, supposedly one of the best in Warsaw. The headwaiter, in a tuxedo, said there were no tables, but one of the waiters scurried up and took my father's arm. "Come this way," he said, glaring at the man in the tuxedo. He put us at a table in the back. My father gave the waiter a 5,000 zloty bill, worth about five American dollars. When the waiter thanked him, my father answered in Polish. We drank Polish vodkas and had a vinegary salad of cucumbers and tomatoes, then a fairly decent slice of beef and boiled potatoes for the main course.

After a disappointing trip to Ostralecko to see the places of his youth, my father lost his enthusiasm for sightseeing and spent several afternoons resting in the hotel, watching television and talking to his broker in the States. I called someone whose number I had brought with me, Tomek Mirkowicz, who had translated the novel of a friend of mine, and he and his wife Julita came by the next afternoon and picked me up at the hotel. They asked me what I wanted to do. "Nothing really," I said. "I just want to see how people live." I asked if they could drive me to their apartment.

"Yes, of course," Julita said. "We're the same way. In America we want to talk to people, but everyone insists on showing us the sights."

We climbed into their small car and drove for half an hour along a winding four-lane road. The trees we passed were tall, with a thin covering of green. They looked like the pictures of trees in the European history text I had studied in high school, trees with a heritage that went back hundreds, thousands of years. It was a sunny day and many people were in the streets. There were especially long lines outside food stores.

"It's right before the weekend, so people are stocking up," Julita said from the back of the car.

They lived in a red brick six-story building that was part of a series of identical buildings. We walked to the fourth floor. The inside of the building was like a high school gym, all grey-colored cement, the staircase and doors unfinished and ugly.

Tomek and Julita had a three-room apartment—a small living room, bedroom and kitchen. The bathroom had a shower and a toilet with a chain for the water tank, which was high on the wall, and a mirror over a tiny sink.

The living room faced the inner courtyard of the project. A gentle breeze blew through the open window, birds chirped, children ran around the paths. The sun shone in on us.

"It's nice and quiet," I said. "In America kids would make more noise."

"It gets noisy here, too," Julita said. "I don't know why it's so quiet today."

Tomek was a tall, slender man in his early thirties with a light brown beard. He wore jeans and white sneakers and a black sweatshirt with "Alcatraz" on it. Julita had on a man's shirt and jeans. Her hair was pulled straight back, and she wore big dark glasses.

I inspected the titles of the books that lined one wall of the living room. Most were American, a number of them by experimental and avant-garde writers that I hadn't read. Tomek had been to America twice and had met many of these writers. It seemed strange to come across someone in Poland who knew more about American literature than most Americans did, though of course that was Tomek's field. Tomek worked at home, translating books from English to Polish. He managed to make a good living working only one or two days a week. "I'm lazy," he said. "I only do my own writing and projects when I feel like it."

Julita also worked as a translator but not solely on literary subjects. She had spent four years in Canada as a young girl. Tomek had grown up in Egypt, where his father served in the Polish consulate. A few abstract paintings on their walls were done by friends, many of whom had little houses in the country where Tomek and Julita often spent weekends away from Warsaw. They had been active in Solidarity, and Julita had been in jail for three weeks the year before when they returned from the U.S. They had known they were in trouble before they came back—that was when Tomek bought his Alcatraz sweatshirt. They'd let a friend of a friend stay at their place while they were away, to water the plants and feed the cat. They realized that he might be someone in hiding, but didn't know who: As it turned out, he was an underground Solidarity leader named Bouriak. Before they got back he was arrested—in their apartment.

"But why did you return at all?" I asked.

"In America I would teach at some small college," Tomek said. "I'd get lost. And I don't want to teach anyway. Here, at least, I make a living translating. Books by Americans sell out in three days. Printings of fifteen thousand. If not for the paper shortage, they could sell fifty thousand."

"And we have our friends and our family," Julita said.

"But the government, the shortages," I asked. ""Doesn't it get you down?"

"You learn not to have certain things," Julita answered. "We read *Newsweek* three weeks late at the American Embassy."

"But that's such a bland magazine."

"Try a Polish magazine instead," Tomek said, smiling.

"There are enough people like us so that we can enjoy ourselves," Julita said. "Painters and writers. And we don't wait on lines. We just don't worry about meat. We eat chicken when we can get it, or vegetables, or whatever's available. Women in Poland have gotten used to waiting on lines. It's part of the day's activity.

"And of course we have no children. And every couple of years we can get out. We might go to Italy soon. Someone from the American Embassy has rented a villa and has given us an open invitation. We'll see if the government will let us go."

Their cat wandered into the room and rubbed against me. I stroked it and it purred. It was a grey cat and had the same smiling expression of the cat of a neighbor of mine in New York, which surprised me, I don't know why. Tomek asked if I minded if he smoked. I said no. It was their house. I didn't like smoking, but smoke seemed a tiny irritation, a luxurious dislike compared to the real possibility of spending years in prison with which they had been threatened.

"Jail was an interesting experience," Julita said. "I discovered they couldn't break me. They told me lies, that Tomek had confessed things that I knew weren't true, and that my father had told them we received money from the underground. That wasn't true either, and my father didn't know anything about us anyway, but I almost believed them. Still, I just stuck to what I knew to be the truth, and they finally let me out. Of course, it was only a month or so. But I feel the stronger for it. And you find out who your real friends are. Certainly my father did. He had been a loyal Communist till then."

A few nights later they had dinner with us at the hotel. My father and I had lamb that was overly salty and dry, and we drank a terrible bottle of Russian wine that the waiter joked about. "Best wine in house," he said, making a face. "Only wine in house." Julita and Tomek both ordered a Chinese dish that I hadn't noticed on the menu. It didn't look much better than the lamb.

Tomek and Julita were particularly nice to my father, attentive to his stories and helpful to him in discussing recent Polish events. They explained why the Jews had been expelled by the Polish government in 1968, after the war in Israel the year before. Sixty thousand Jews returned from Russia after the Second World War, but when the Communists sided with Egypt in '67, the Polish government, in support of the Russians, expelled the Jews. Neither my father nor I knew that Jews had ever returned to Poland. Tomek and Julita talked calmly and informatively, and I trusted their objectivity and intelligence. Being with them gave me a feeling of oneness with the world, that there were intelligent, humane people in all countries, something easy for me to forget, particularly in Poland with its history of anti-Semitism.

A few days later my father and I boarded a Lufthansa plane to Frankfort, on our way to Cannes, where my brother's in-laws lived, and my father's mood began to improve. The stewardess served big sandwiches and plied my father with drinks. I was stuffed from all the heavy Polish food and didn't eat anything. But on the flight to Cannes, I finished everything and drank some, too.

In Cannes my father's leg hurt him even worse than in Poland, for which he blamed the sea air. He'd forgotten all the effort it took to get through airports. Of course on his previous trip fifteen years before, he'd had more strength and he had been with his mistress, a thirty-year-old stewardess. He talked about her all the time. "I was strong then," he told me. "Not like now. I can't do it anymore," he said. "Maybe I could if the woman was right, but I don't know."

He looked at women in the streets and in the lobby. "That one could kill you," he said of a woman in shorts with a big rear end.

"Not a bad way to go," I said. We were teenagers walking the neighborhood.

I held his arm as he hobbled across the street to one of the wooden seats facing the Mediterranean. It was the middle of May, chilly for swimming, so the beach wasn't crowded, but many people passed along the esplanade. "There's one like me," my father said of an old man with a cane. The difference was the old man was walking with an old woman. My father didn't want to walk with an old woman.

We crossed back to our hotel and went upstairs to read the paper. I put on the television and watched the French Open. The reception was clear and the camera coverage wonderfully close up. I looked in on my father several times. He was sleeping with his mouth open, breathing with a raspy, old man's sound.

That night I had a nightmare, a variation of one I'd been having since I was small. Robbers were coming through the door to our hotel room. I started to scream and woke up in a sweat. My father reached over from his bed alongside and took my hand. "It's all right, darling," he said. "I'm here. Everything's all right."

We came back to New York a few days early, and I was depressed the first week I was home. I blamed it on my being a bad traveler, the time change, and my father's poor health in Europe; and my realization that he was an old man . But I knew it wasn't just that. I found myself thinking of the sunny view from Tomek and Julita's apartment. Their life seemed so easy going. It was the kind of life I daydreamed about. Shopping at four or five for a casual dinner. Lying around reading, making love in the afternoon. Picnics in the country with friends. Julita had said that she missed good apples. The apples in Poland, like everything else imported from Russia, were soft and tasteless. I wished I were allowed to send her a barrel of apples. Instead I put together a shipment of books and magazines and a letter thanking her and Tomek for their kindness.

Ostralecko

My father was actually born twenty miles north of Ostralecko, in Gunteretz, which he also wanted to see, but our travel agent in New York had advised against going because Gunteretz was so small it wasn't even on the map and the roads looked impassable. If we got stuck overnight the only accommodations there would be primitive, so we decided against it. My father was eighty-six at the time, though still vigorous and overpowering, at least to me. We had first flown to Paris on the Concorde in a package deal, which gave us a free room for one night in a famous old hotel whose name I forget. We arrived late at night and were taken to our room, which looked like any ordinary hotel room, and my father told the bellhop he wasn't happy with the accommodations.

"I was here in '72 in a suite with my girlfriend Sally," he told me. "And that's the kind of room I want."

I accompanied him to the front desk and he told the manager his problem.

"But this is part of the package," the manager explained.

My father described the suite he'd had in 1972, and the manager told him that was impossible, it would cost an additional one thousand dollars.

"I'll take it," my father said.

I tried to tell him that it was crazy to pay that kind of money for one night, but my father put up his hand.

"Don't tell me what to do. I'm an old man. I'll live my life as I want to. I stayed in a suite in 1972 and I'll stay in one now."

He did tell me that the suite had been much cheaper then. American dollars weren't going very far in '87. After we moved to our suite we went down to the hotel bar for coffee and a sandwich. The bill came to eighty dollars. Things had changed since '72.

The next day we flew to Frankfort and then to Warsaw. We stayed at the fanciest hotel in the city, which resembled a large cheap hotel off a U.S highway. My father wasn't very happy there. On the second day Jerzy, our guide, drove us to Ostralecko. My father was searching for a tree he had planted in 1911. He remembered exactly where it was. In fact, he remembered the names of the families and the location of his neighbors' houses. And after sixty-five years he was also able to speak Polish with what Jerzy said was a perfect accent.

As we approached Ostralecko we were surrounded by overhead wires and oil tanks. Ostralecko looked something like the area around Newark along the New Jersey Turnpike.

When we got to the town square my father recognized nothing. His tree wasn't there and none of the houses were either. Only the Catholic Church remained standing. Everything else was gone, and the Russians had rebuilt the town with ugly, depressing, flimsily constructed houses and factories. It was drizzling out and we never left the car.

"It's all gone," my father said, and told Jerzy to turn around and go back to Warsaw. I wanted to go the bathroom, but my father seemed so desperate to get away that I sat two hours in the gloom and waited until we reached our hotel.

My father didn't say much on the return trip, and when we got back he took a long nap. His spirits picked up at the hotel restaurant at dinner, and he kept looking at a very attractive, well-groomed woman in her mid-fifties eating by herself at a nearby table. A harpist was playing old popular romantic American songs like "My Funny Valentine" and "All the Things You Are."

"She's alone," my father said. "I think I saw her looking at us. Maybe

I'll invite her to join us and see what happens."

I knew he was still dispirited from our visit to Ostralecko, but I didn't want to watch my eighty-six-year-old father try to pick up a younger woman.

"I'm almost finished with dinner," I told him. "I'll go out to the lobby and wait for you."

I sat in an armchair in the lobby and watched groups of Germans and Poles, who were there for a health conference, mill around.

My father appeared fifteen minutes later. He hadn't made his move, he told me. I'm not sure if it was because he sensed my disapproval or because he'd lost his confidence.

The next day he complained about the poverty and the long lines we kept seeing as we drove around Warsaw. "It used to be so beautiful. It was known as Little Paris. Now it's in ruins." He said his leg hurt and started walking with a limp.

We left a day early for Cannes. We stayed in a beautiful hotel facing the beach and ate with my brother's in-laws at expensive restaurants and inns.

By the time we were ready to return to the States my father was joking about his trip to Ostralecko and the woman he had wanted to pick up in the restaurant. He talked about going back to Poland the next year, this time trying to reach Gunteretz and going to the house where he'd been born.

On the flight back he flirted with the stewardess, telling her she looked very much like his old girlfriend Sally, who was also a stewardess. During the last part of the trip she knelt in the aisle next to us and talked with my father. She seemed interested in getting together with him in New York and asked where he lived, but my father didn't respond to her hints.

"She's not my type," he said in the car on the way back from Kennedy. "Probably thinks she can get some money from me."

I think he preferred being the aggressor, but I could tell he was pleased by her interest.

More About My Mother and Father

My father was remarkably aware and lively right till the last minute, expressing interest in front page articles in the *New York Times*. Doctors and nurses enjoyed being with him, and extended their bedside visits to listen to his stories, such as how he sold lemonade along the road to the Russian soldiers when they occupied Poland in 1914. The Russian recruits didn't know their left from their right, and wore a piece of straw on one shoulder so the commander could give instructions by saying, To the side with the straw, turn! Near the end I knew most of his stories and when we were alone I used to ask him to tell me one.

He had come to America from Poland with no money, so for him everything revolved around building a successful business and moving up in the world. Dinner out was in the garment district where he could meet business colleagues and make connections. In the last years of his life he became more speculative and seemed to be looking over his past, summing things up, trying to understand human nature. But he wasn't a man to second-guess himself. I never heard him say he shouldn't have married my mother. What was done was done: all his effort to get ahead, all his philandering, that's what a man had to do. Make money and satisfy his needs.

His father had been in the lumber business on land near their house. The family lived a rural life, raising most of their own food. His father's workers came to the house once a week to be paid, and my father remembered him distributing, with each worker's wages, a small amount of tobacco. The next day the house would still smell of it. My grandfather liked to vacation at a German spa every year, and when the Russians invaded in 1914 they accused him of being a spy for the Germans. Russian soldiers dug his grave and were going to shoot him, until a neighboring landlord vouched for him. The Russians motioned to him to go home, but he thought they were pointing toward the firing squad and he was never the same afterwards. Later on, after my father brought him to New York, my grandfather used to cross the street at the sight of a policeman.

My grandfather and grandmother had nineteen children. "Did he have girlfriends, too?" I asked my father jokingly. "No, he wasn't that type of man," my father said. "He was very serious. My mother, too. She was a small woman, never said anything bad about anybody."

My father was the second youngest of the children; many of the oldest ones moved away as he was growing up so he didn't get to know them. By the time he was born the family was fairly well off. There were no schools for Jewish children where he lived, so he had to travel to get an education. School consisted of sitting with other pupils around a table and studying the Talmud. "I was a good student," my father told me. "I had a photographic memory. I remembered everything that was important and ignored the rest so I wouldn't clutter my mind. Sometimes I had to sleep on the floor of the family I stayed with, but I didn't mind. I was young and strong and wanted to learn."

When he was eighteen he was drafted into the Polish army. He worked in a supply company. "I had a good handwriting and the captain liked me," he told me. "I carried a toothbrush with me wherever I went and used to brush my teeth after every meal. The captain asked me what made us Jewboys so clean. He wanted to promote me, but he said I had to change my name from Abe to one that sounded more Polish." Despite his fondness for wearing a uniform and riding a horse, my father decided that a Jew in the Polish army didn't have a promising future, so he forged papers sending him to Germany.

After living six months in Germany, then going to Cuba, where he spent another eight months, he managed to get to America in 1921, arriving by boat in Florida with Cuban papers under the name of Anthony Salgado. At immigration he immediately changed his name back to Schrader and took a train to New York City. Even though I asked him a number of times, he never satisfactorily explained how he was able to discard his assumed name without legal problems.

"When I got to New York," he said. "I took a look around and knew I could be a success. All you had to do was work hard and use your brains."

At twenty-two he started working in the dress business. His first job was delivering dresses for a contractor. Once when he was pushing a load of dresses up Seventh Avenue it began to snow, and he took off his coat and covered the hand truck to keep the dresses from getting wet. When the owner, Morris Halft, one of the biggest manufacturers at the time, saw him uncover the dresses, he thanked him and told him he would go far in business. During the Depression, when my father had progressed to being a contractor, he learned how to save fabric by helping his cutters rearrange the dress patterns (which the manufacturers supplied), thus producing an extra dress or two for his own profit while still delivering the required number of dresses to the manufacturer.

During the Second World War he manufactured WAC uniforms. He had to pay off someone at the Woolen Association to get fabric, which was rationed. "That's what you had to do to succeed," he told me.

Only three of my father's sisters came to America from their small town in Poland. My mother was from Warsaw, and because she had gone to school there, she considered herself more cultured than my father's sisters. The sisters had kept their heavy Yiddish accents, while my mother and, to a lesser degree, my father, managed to lose theirs thanks to the speech classes they took in night school, which is where they met.

Late in life my mother used to tell me about her admirers before she married my father. She left Poland at seventeen with her younger sister Faye. In Paris my mother worked in a doll factory and advanced quickly because of her skill in sewing. She and Faye were beautiful young women with delicate features. My mother was short, with a full bosom and light brown hair and blue eyes. Faye was tall, with red hair and a model's figure. The boss's son proposed to my mother, but she refused him. He wasn't Jewish and anyway she wanted to come to America. She and Faye reached New York after eight months in Paris. My mother worked in a factory, took English classes at night, and studied painting at the Academy of Fine Arts. Faye enrolled in public school and advanced five grades in a year. She read everything she could and wrote poetry. An instructor at the Fine Arts Academy tried to court my mother, but she thought he wouldn't earn a decent living as an artist. Also he was blond, which she felt would make their children too fair.

Then she met my father. They learned poems and tongue twisters and speeches together in speech class. They were married in City Hall and Faye moved in with them. But my father didn't get along with Faye, who was overly dependent on my mother, and when Faye moved to Chicago my mother gradually lost touch with her.

My mother remained beautiful all her life, heavier in middle age, then thin again in old age, her features delicate, her skin clear and unlined.

During the last ten or twelve years of her life, in her deep depression and mostly staying in bed, she would raise her head when she saw me and repeat one of her sayings, something like, "Time goes by with heartbreaking swiftness," and then, pleased with herself, she'd smile and lie back on her pillow.

Eating Separately

Soon after my father married my mother, he developed a sensitive stomach, supposedly due to her lack of cooking skills. One of the first meals she served him was a chicken so undercooked that he had to spit mouthfuls into his napkin when she wasn't looking. Eventually my mother learned the art of cooking, at least the basics, and if her dishes weren't overly appetizing, they were at least edible—steak, roast beef, chopped meat, liver, plain salads of iceberg lettuce, Jell-O. Her specialties were matzo brie during Passover and jelly cookies around Christmas time. My mother's life centered on cooking, and her main interaction with the outside world occurred when she shopped for food. She had a suspicious nature and felt everyone was out to cheat her; she insisted on going to the back of the store with her butcher to watch him grind meat for her so that he wouldn't substitute a cheaper cut.

But by the time I got to high school we ate fewer and fewer meals as a family. My father and older brother rarely came home till late and in 1952, after her hysterectomy, my mother spent the winter by herself at Dr. Max Warmbrand's spa in Orlando, Florida. Dr. Warmbrand, who wrote books about food and was something of a pre-New Age guru, lectured to his guests about how to live wisely and happily. He was married to his ex-wife's sister, with whom he'd had an affair while still married. My mother shook her head at such goings on, but she gave geniuses a special leeway. Every morning she would take a walk to pick oranges from the spa's orange grove, and would feed a few to Dr. Warmbrand's dog, which would accompany her. She also engaged in long conversations with the nuns from the convent next door. My mother would have been happy as a nun, crocheting and knitting all day and dwelling on spiritual matters, and she returned from Florida with newly found serenity. She prepared more imaginative dishes, like a squash casserole with chunks of pineapple mixed in for flavor, and she seemed more relaxed. She had a sweet tooth and used honey in nearly everything she made. Mostly she ate vegetables and fish, though she still occasionally liked to indulge in eating meat, which she bought at an expensive East Side market.

She had developed many rules at the table over the years—food had to be eaten hot, right out of the oven, otherwise the vitamins disappeared into the air; drinking water during a meal washed the food down and took away its nutritional value and was bad for digestion; certain foods fought in the stomach and shouldn't be eaten together, though the forbidden combinations changed arbitrarily.

When my father came home late, my mother was always ready to prepare a meal for him in case he hadn't eaten enough earlier. If he did agree to have something, she would prepare it quickly and then stand at the door of the dining room and silently watch him eat. But after a while she couldn't refrain from asking if everything was all right, if the fish was overcooked, if the vegetables tasted fresh. My father would be listening to the small radio that he kept on the table, his back to her, and would say in an irritated way that everything was fine but that he needed silence to concentrate on the news.

Later, privately, he would complain to me about my mother, that her whole life was centered on food, and that he couldn't talk to her about business or politics or life in general. Yet he also had mixed feelings about more worldly, successful women, and often made critical comments about their appearance. Much later in life, watching Secretary of State Madeleine Albright on television, he said to me, "Look at the size of her ass," as if that negated her ability to carry out foreign policy. His critique of Hillary Clinton was that her legs were thick enough to hold up a piano.

By the time she was in her early seventies, my mother could barely cook or shop, and she wandered around the house in her bathrobe, talking to herself. Her eyesight was failing and she was unable to knit or crochet, something she'd done since childhood and had taken great pleasure and pride in. My father now ate exclusively at four-star French restaurants like Caravelle and Le Cirque, usually inviting a friend or two for company. He insisted on his food being prepared simply, the way he liked it—baked fish with no oil, burned on the outside, and steamed vegetables. He could be demanding and critical about the food and the service, but the waiters seemed to admire him for his determination and his humor and his elegant attire and his large tips. Each time he visited a restaurant he'd slip a twenty dollar bill to the maitre d', so he always sat at one of the preferred tables in the front, near to whichever celebrities were out the same night—anyone from Nixon to Joe Namath—and my father invariably would start a conversation. He told former President Nixon that he had admired his foreign policy, especially with China, and Nixon thanked him for his praise. In the Sixties, my father got to know Johnson and Humphrey and visited them frequently in the White House. He described them as big drinkers and said they had girlfriends—according to him, all successful, important men had mistresses. Once at a party at the White House my father was dancing with the young attractive wife of a cabinet minister, and Johnson, who towered over my father, put his arm around him and nearly lifted him off the floor and told him it was time to change partners. Johnson was having an affair with her, my father said.

Sometimes I wondered if he was exaggerating when he told me of all the famous people he met and how they had become his good friends, but at a party at Gracie Mansion that he took me to, Lauren Bacall walked over to him and kissed him warmly and told him how good it was to see him again. Later, when I asked about her, he hardly seemed to remember her or to even be aware of what an icon she was.

As my mother aged, she deteriorated and grew more peculiar and out of touch with the world, while my father continued to thrive. They were like a variation of Oscar Wilde's *The Picture of Dorian Gray*—my mother aging at home while my father remained youthful in the outside world. My mother suffered from a variety of painful symptoms—a perpetual feeling of nausea, a burning in her urinary tract, and a constant fatigue. With little to distract her, she became obsessed with death, convinced she didn't have long to go, and lived that way for the rest of her life, nearly twenty years. My father continued to go out every night. He was still able to get on the dance floor at formal dinners and flirt with his partners. When my father was eighty-five, Mayor Koch honored him with a ceremony at City Hall and declared it Abe Schrader Day. My father's main concession to age was to get up a little later in the morning, and then prepare for the day in a leisurely manner. He'd use a suppository (something he'd done every day since he was twenty-five), shower and shave, and then eat breakfast and listen to the news. At exactly ten he'd call his broker and write down the prices of the shares of the dozen or so stocks he had large amounts invested in. He would look at the *New York Times* and the *New York Post* and begin getting dressed. Then he'd call one of his cronies to set up a dinner appointment and finally, a little after eleven, go downstairs and settle comfortably in the back seat of his car and be driven to work by his chauffeur.

In 1988 my mother died of a heart attack. She hadn't felt well during the day, but insisted the maid not disturb my father at work. Finally, late in the afternoon, the maid called him and he rushed home, but by then my mother was unconscious. He rode in the ambulance to the hospital with her and urged the doctors in the emergency room to do everything to keep her alive, even after they told him there was no hope. The doctors made an incision and tried to stimulate her heart but soon she was dead. My father was overcome with grief. "Why didn't they call me right away," he kept repeating. "I could have kept her alive."

He remained in the dress business until he was eighty-nine, when he was forced out by the conglomerate that had bought his company five years before. For a year or so he stayed home and traded stocks over the phone through his broker. When I visited him in the afternoon he'd still be in the bedroom, unshaven, wearing his bathrobe, looking at a business channel on television and following the ticker tape of stocks that rolled by on the bottom of the screen. It was the only time I knew him when he wasn't busy rushing off to work or to the track or to a poker game, and he would encourage me to stay and talk.

But when his broker retired, my father decided to go to Wall Street and trade for himself. He sat at a desk in a brokerage office, following the stock prices on the TV screen and jotting down numbers. If he got tired he would put his head down and take a nap. He enjoyed the company of the other people at the brokerage. The man in the lobby who shined his shoes every morning called him Abe. My father followed this routine until his doctor called in late May 2001 to tell him that his blood tests looked suspicious. This occurred during a severe recession in the stock market, and my father seemed as upset at the prospect of dying in the midst of large financial losses as he was at the thought of death itself. But six weeks later when he died, the market was even further down. His time had run out.

Talking to My Father

After my mother tried to commit suicide for the second time, I asked the family doctor to recommend a nursing home, and a week later my father and I traveled to Westchester to visit one. My father went under protest. "I'll never put her away," he said. "I would never do that to her." The nursing home turned out to be a disaster. The first thing we saw inside were several deranged-looking old people making faces and odd frightening sounds, walking bent over or strapped into chairs so they wouldn't fall out. My father was furious with me on the trip back. "That's where you want to send your mother? That's how much you love her?"

I told him I agreed with him about this particular home, but that I still thought Mother wasn't in a good situation, that she felt like a failure because she was so tired all the time and could no longer fulfill what she considered were her obligations to him and to the house.

"I've got plenty of maids," my father said. "They can take care of the house."

"But she's unhappy that the maids do all the work now." There was no explaining my mother's depression to him. He was deaf to my criticism that he never spoke to her and that he chased her from the dining room if she came in while he was eating.

I tried to tell him that she wasn't normal anymore, and that this was why I suggested placing her in a nursing home. "You're telling *me* she's not normal?" he said. And he went through a litany of complaints covering the last fifty years. The two of them were not likely candidates for couples therapy, so aside from visiting my mother frequently, I gave up trying to mediate.

When my mother died six years later, my father and I became more friendly and relaxed together. I think he mellowed at the realization that he was alone and that, at eighty-eight, his own death was imminent. With my mother no longer around to incense him, I began to appreciate his good qualities. He was funny and lively and generous, always making the best of situations, including his old age. As he approached ninety, women he met were still attracted by his charm and flirtatiousness, and he enjoyed their attention.

I asked him about Mother. Had they ever gotten along? "Yes, at the beginning," he said. "She was very beautiful. We had passionate sex."

"When did you start playing around?" I asked.

"Pretty early," he said. "But my first real affair was with Helen, my forelady. Her husband was a policeman, and he did something wrong and was sent to jail for a couple of years. It was the best sex I ever had."

I remembered Helen, a big homely Polish woman who inspected dresses in the factory with a mean, critical eye, and I was shocked.

"Was she your girlfriend? Did you go out together?"

"No, we were both married. When everybody left at night we used to have sex on the cutting room table."

"When was that?"

"Around 1932."

Nineteen thirty-two was the year my brother was born, two years before my sister Estelle died, and three years before I was born. I imagined that when my father grew up in Europe men played around, though never seriously. You didn't leave your wife for a girlfriend. Divorce wasn't a possibility, though I don't think my father ever thought about finding another partner.

In his nineties my father talked frequently about sex, how he could barely get an erection. All he wanted to do now, he said, was to make money in the stock market. He spent every day at the brokerage house on Wall Street, trading his own portfolio. There were several Orthodox Jewish traders in the firm, and he discussed the Talmud with them. He'd been educated in yeshivas and loved to show his knowledge, though he wasn't a believer. With the other brokers he talked stocks and tried to pick up tips. He flirted with the secretaries, who loved to tease him. One of them used to sit in his lap and tell him how much she was attracted to him. She'd put her hand inside his pants and goose him. "That Sharon's something," he said. "Drives me crazy. If only she wasn't married."

Every six months or so a woman friend visited from Florida. He told me she was around fifty, wealthy and attractive. She'd been married to an older man who had died and left her with money. My father would take her out to dinner and then bring her back to his apartment (always on his housekeeper's night out). The next few days he'd strut around like an old rooster with his chest out. "I can still do it," he'd boast to his friends. "I'm not finished yet."

But near the end of his life he stopped seeing her. "She's stupid," he said. "I've got nothing to talk to her about. Politics, the world. She's ignorant."

I realized that he had never liked any of his girlfriends. They had all been common or greedy or had some grievous fault. The dancing instructor with the interest in existentialism had become a drug addict. The stewardess with the voluptuous body turned out to be nasty and greedy. My father wanted to be seen with attractive younger women and have sex with them, but then eventually get rid of them. My mother was the only one he didn't get rid of. She was the mother of his children, and he endured her as best he could.

My father was full of contradictions. He could speak five languages and was well educated in history and philosophy. He had a photographic memory and, though he didn't read much once he came to America, he could discuss in detail novels he'd read in the 1920's, like *Anna Karenina* and *An American Tragedy*. He was a generous giver to hospitals and charities, and was known and revered by hundreds of people he met around town. But his narcissism and ambition kept him from wanting a deep connection with a woman. A woman would only have gotten in his way. Unfortunately for her, my mother was that woman.

Last Visit

I arrive at my father's hospital room at about 11:10 PM.

"Kisses, kisses, I need kisses," he says, big pauses between his words. I kiss his cheek several times. He takes my hand and lifts the oxygen mask and kisses my hand and holds it tightly.

"You and Mort love each other. Don't fight. I loved my sons, my family. I loved every minute of it."

He's very uncomfortable, gasping for breath. A big fan is right next to him, blowing at high speed, but he wants more air. He keeps trying to pull off the oxygen mask. The night nurse Ellenita and I keep putting it back over his mouth. I tell him he was a wonderful father, that everyone loves him and is asking for him, that everyone at the hospital loves him.

"It's no good," he says, "I'm causing my family trouble." He makes a sweeping gesture with his hands to show it's over, that he's dying. He grows increasingly uneasy and it becomes harder for him to speak. He asks what day it is and I tell him it's late Wednesday, nearly midnight.

"Make it Sunday, no, Monday," he says, giving me instructions for his funeral. "Make it big. And big in the *New York Times*."

He thrashes around, gasping for air and pulling the mask off. Lourdes, the nurse for the early morning shift, comes on and calls someone else in to change his position so that he can breathe easier.

I walk out of the room and down the hall to get a drink of water. When I come back I see an extra nurse by the bed. I think she is there to pull my father up on the bed toward the pillows, but she is the head nurse and is checking to see if he is breathing. She shakes her head and she and Lourdes begin to loosen the packing on my father's legs, which helped his circulation. I realize that he has died. It is about 12:30. In a while several attending doctors arrive and pronounce him dead officially at 12:50 AM.

Rainy, Cold Days

At ninety-five my father complained about rainy, cold days, though he would always go to work anyway. The weather got in his bones, he said, made him sad and made him think of death.

My father put his shoes on before his pants. When I asked him why, he said he just did it that way, just as every night he counted his money, which he kept in a silver money clip and put in a drawer next to his bed.

When the doctor called on a Friday night after receiving the results of his blood test and told him to go to the hospital immediately, my father sensed it was the beginning of the end. His accountant Rona had been laid off at the firm's office that day, and he was upset because she was the only one who understood his complicated finances. Also, it had been a terrible day in the stock market, and in the cab on the way to the hospital he kept saying that the evil eye was on him—three bad things had happened in one day, an unlucky number. Evil eye was an expression from his childhood, and I felt he was slipping back in his mind to Gunteretz.

Not long before he died, I asked my father if he believed in God or in an afterlife. "No," he said, "This is all there is."

In his last few years he became mellower and grew closer to my brother and me. We were two sides of him. With me he quoted writers and told stories of his childhood. With my brother he discussed business and money.

Sitting in the movies with me when I was about nine, he asked me if I loved him more than I loved my mother. "I love you both the same,"

I said. "But I love you a little more than your brother," he said. "Well, maybe I love you a little more," I told him. He squeezed my hand and we went back to watching the movie.

In one of my earliest memories, my parents took Mort to the World's Fair in 1939 and left me behind with a sitter. Children needed to be five years old to be allowed in, they said. I wasn't quite four. After they left I cried for a long time, but when they came home they brought presents from the Fair for me and told me all about the exhibits showing the future of the world, and I felt happy, almost as if I had gone myself.

Recently I asked my brother why he had split up with his first wife forty years ago and he said, "I never think about things like that, I think about today, maybe yesterday. I think about what I'm going to do, not what I did."

How can we be so different? I think about the past all the time, probably too much. Yet I love my brother and want his approval the way I did my father's. Of course, it's not there. Like my father, he's a preoccupied man.

My father's funeral was on the 13th of the month and my brother paid for it with his credit card, thinking the charge would come through the following month, like with a store or restaurant. Two days later, though, when the credit card bill came the funeral expenses appeared there. The funeral chapel was not going to wait a month to be paid and must have called it in the same day. It seemed a little cold-blooded to me, but I imagine that my father, as a businessman, would have respected what they did.

Since My Father Died

My father seemed like such a powerful man that I felt he would go on forever, which in a way he almost did, since he died at one hundred. I think he sometimes had the feeling he would outlive my brother and me. He often told me how my brother went out too much, worked too hard, and didn't take care of himself. He and my brother had been in business together for over thirty-five years and competed head on. I admired my brother for standing up to him when they disagreed, something I knew I couldn't do.

My father put up such a strong front it was hard to realize just how old and fragile he had become in his last years. At the end, when he died of complications from an operation for colon cancer, his doctor told me that his intestines were like tissue paper.

In his last days he knew he was dying and talked of how much he loved my brother and me. Yet he was still demanding. He rang impatiently for a nurse at his slightest need and was critical of the staff. It wasn't until the last weeks that he allowed my brother to sign checks for him. Near the end he insisted my brother wasn't taking care of things properly, and he tried to transfer more money to his checking account despite my brother's assurance that there were sufficient funds left. "He doesn't know anything," my father said to me through his oxygen mask, and made a dismissive motion with his hand.

He had tubes and machines attached to him all over his body and arms, and his legs were swollen with liquid because he wasn't able to urinate. Once he asked me where he was. "Beth Israel Hospital," I told him. "I don't understand," he said. "I was just in Poland." Still, he was coherent enough to make the decision to be operated on, so that he would have the chance to live without tubes in him.

The day of the surgery I visited him at six in the morning and found him holding forth to the operating team of ten or so young doctors who had come to accompany him from his room. He was telling them about his life, quoting from Nietzsche or at least something he attributed to him, then the Talmud, and then a Jewish folk tale. He pointed to one of the young doctors, a blonde. "She's from Brooklyn," he told me. "Cute, isn't she?" The group was spellbound. They had never operated on anyone one hundred years old. I barely had time to kiss him and say goodbye and wish him well.

The operation didn't help. Advanced cancer was discovered. He wouldn't get the time he wanted to make back the money he'd lost in the market that year. His kidney became infected and his body broke down. He would have lived longer had he left the cancer alone, but that wasn't his way. He was a hard-driving, gregarious man, and he didn't want to live with tubes in him.

Often I wished I was from a less pressured, less ambitious, less successful, more loving family. At restaurants my father had to be up front so he could greet people and be seen. He loved the rich and famous. He was always getting up during a meal and talking to someone he knew. He was an immigrant from Poland who'd made good and palled around with politicians and millionaires. In his view, opinions didn't have authority unless they were validated by someone successful and rich. He still worried about his Jewish accent. When I was younger I wanted a father who would take pleasure in me for my own qualities and not because any success of mine would shed additional glory on him.

Since my father died my brother and I see each other more often. When my father was alive we used to hear about each other through him. He was the conduit.

Since my father died I feel liberated, more myself. I know he liked my company and I used to have a good time with him, but when we were out together I felt as if I was always having to flatter his vanity. He always had to be right, and my job was to appreciate him and make him feel good. I was an expert in this. I knew most of his stories and experiences and his likes and dislikes. I went with him to restaurants and to dinners and to doctors' offices. If he had to make an after-dinner speech for a charity, I wrote one out for him, which he depended on because he wasn't confident about his English and his accent. I tried to explain to him that his accent and his firsthand knowledge of history and religion were what made him a successful speaker, but he didn't believe me. He needed something written out as security, then he could be spontaneous.

When I wrote a first draft for him, he would read it out loud and immediately tell me my mistakes—he'd come to America in 1921, not 1920, as I had written. He never thanked me. It wasn't his way. A public appearance was so important it took precedence over manners. He was a man of enormous ego, perhaps good for a businessman, but not a wonderful quality in a father. It wasn't until I was in my fifties that I developed enough confidence in myself to accept that in him. Then I enjoyed being able to help him, and when I saw how other people struggled with their parents in nursing homes, I appreciated my father's vitality. He walked with a bounce right till the end and didn't complain.

I helped him write checks the last few years of his life when the secretary who came to his apartment once a month grew too old and sickly to work. A dozen or so bills would be piled in front of him—rent, phone bill, restaurants, housekeeper, chauffeur, car rental, garage. He'd hand me one bill at a time and I'd write out the check and he'd inspect it against the bill before signing it and putting a stamp on the envelope. His inspection took a long time and I made more mistakes than I normally would have. I felt he was right on top of me, breathing on me almost.

I miss him, but I also feel free.

Estelle

Just before he died, in the middle of a discussion about the mildness of winter weather over the last few years, my father told me that on the day of Estelle's funeral the Hudson River was already frozen. This was at the end of October 1934.

My sister Estelle died at seven, a year before I was born and, as I was growing up, my parents hardly ever spoke about her. From what relatives told me, I learned that she had died from an infection in her nose, incorrectly diagnosed, that spread within a few days to her brain. This was before drugs like penicillin. I can remember my mother telling me two incidents about Estelle. Once she came home from school in tears because a bunch of kids taunted her in the schoolyard, saying that the Jews killed Christ. Another time Estelle was across the street with Mort, who was almost five years younger, and some older boys grabbed him and passed him over the schoolyard fence and then back over to the street. This was dangerous because the fence was high and the boys had to hold on with one hand while they passed Mort from one to the other. Estelle was around six or seven then, so it's hard to know how aware she was of the danger. These are the only two stories I remember hearing, though Estelle's name occasionally came up in conversation.

After my father died I found, buried deep in a closet, a cardboard box with mementos and pictures of Estelle. One of the items in the box was a school loose-leaf notebook. The first page is entitled "Pleasant Stories," but the material that follows is mostly beginning handwriting exercises. Then there are several drawings in colored pencil, done, I am sure, by my mother, as they are precise and detailed, the kind my mother drew for me when I first went to school, and for my son Daniel when he was little. After a few blank pages there is a child's drawing, presumably by Estelle, of a girl in a blue dress with yellow and blue hair and a red mouth, a brown circle for a nose, and two red spots on her cheek. There are no legs but each blue arm has five red lines for fingers.

In addition, Estelle made a little booklet of brown paper tied together with a faded orange-brownish ribbon, called "A Bouquet for My Mother," which has six pages of crayon drawings of flowers.

Then there are loose papers from P.S. 187, mostly spelling and math quizzes, and several beginning compositions written on small pieces of lined paper, cut from a larger page, the kind distributed in class by the teacher.

On September 20 she wrote: My name is Estelle Schrader. I am in Class 2A.

And on October 18: We should take good care of health. We should eat vegetables to make them grow strong.

And by the end of the month she had died.

Her medical bills, addressed to my parents on Northern Avenue (which later became Cabrini Boulevard) and also stored in the box, came to sixty-two dollars.

My father had no money at the time, so the bills must have been difficult for him. This was the middle of the Depression, and when I was born a year later he was behind several months' rent on his business loft and also on his apartment. At the time people moved from place to place in order to get several months' free rent from landlords, who were desperate for tenants. This may explain why my parents had moved a few blocks away from Northern Avenue to 660 Fort Washington Avenue; though maybe it was just too painful for them to remain in the apartment where Estelle had died. It couldn't have been a good time— a severe early winter with the Hudson frozen and my father broke. I imagine the only reason for having another child in such conditions was to replace Estelle, so in a way I owe my existence to her death.

The most vivid images of Estelle are the ten or so photos in the cardboard box. Five photos, dated September 1929, when Estelle was two, were taken at the beach, probably Rockaway, where we later went in the summer when I was small.

My mother and father sit in the sand. Estelle is on my mother's lap, looking away. My mother's and father's arms are touching. In another photo they are both holding Estelle, who has one foot on my mother's leg and one on my father's. My parents are smiling.

Three photos show my father sitting in the water at the shore holding Estelle on his lap, both of them smiling. My father is wearing an old-style tank top bathing suit. A lock of hair comes down over his forehead. He is twenty-eight, young and handsome.

Part VI   Flying to Minnesota

Birthday

My birthday came on a Friday this year, and my wife Alice had to be away in Troy, New York, for the weekend at a workshop for a film organization whose board she serves on. My wife is a fairly obsessive worker, and on Friday morning she was so preoccupied with packing and making sure that her ninety-year-old father (who lives alone and has recently been ill) had sufficient care for the weekend that she forgot what day it was or even to kiss me goodbye. I always claim that I don't like the sentimentality of birthdays, and we had already celebrated on Wednesday night with my brother and son and their wives, so the festivities were sort of taken care of. But I still felt sad at her going away, though I said nothing and wished her a good trip as she got into the elevator.

I was sixty-six and couldn't pin down exactly how I felt. Some days I was droopy and slow, other days lively and alert, seemingly much younger than my chronological age. Maybe that was part of the aging process—big shifts in mood and energy, a sort of AC/DC high or low where you can go either way.

I had an appointment for a checkup with Dr. Mizrachi, the radiation oncologist who had treated me a few months before for prostate cancer. My symptoms from the radiation had pretty much disappeared, and I wasn't nervous about the visit. In fact, I was looking forward to seeing Dr. Mizrachi again. He's a young, dynamic, cheerful person who is always bursting with energy and life, despite being surrounded all day by suffering and illness.

I took my usual route to the Beth Israel Center at Union Square—the 7th Avenue local to 14th Street—exited at the front of the station, and then walked east on 12th Street, one of my favorite areas, past well-preserved brownstones, St Vincent's Hospital, the New School, and the Cinema Village Theater where I checked the marquee to see if anything interesting was playing. Last spring I did this for forty-two consecutive days, excluding weekends and Memorial Day. The weather had been nearly perfect, with only one rainy day. I felt nostalgic now as I strolled along, reminded of an illness I had been through and seemingly survived, ready for old age, though aware more than previously that there were no guarantees. My appointment was a routine one to see how I was doing and to take a sample of my blood.

I said hello to Sandra, the receptionist, who barely seemed to remember me. The waiting room was fairly empty and I didn't have to wait long. A nurse led me to an examination room and asked me questions, writing my answers out on a form. She asked me about my energy level, the frequency of my urination, and my sexual function. I generally answer these questions as positively as I can, partly because I usually feel good during examinations and also partly because I feel superstitious, hoping somehow that the less I complain the better I'll eventually feel. The nurse had to stick me twice before she was able to get a sufficient blood sample, but she was sweet and apologetic and I didn't mind.

Soon Dr. Mizrachi bounded in, wearing his usual dark shirt and bright tie. He's a small man in his early forties, bald with black sideburns, and thin and wiry, looking as if he goes to the gym regularly. He is, I believe, of Iranian Jewish background. "It's quiet today," I told him.

"Yes, I'm working fast because I'll be on a plane to Italy in six hours."

Dr. Mizrachi loves Italy and goes there as often as he can. He has told me repeatedly that he likes to reward himself for working hard, and feels patients should do the same after they complete treatment

"Did you take a vacation when you finished here last summer?" he asked.

"Yes, I went to Vermont," I told him, though I didn't add that I went for only a short time because my father died in July.

"How's sex?" he asked.

I knew from reading that statistically most men will be finished sexually within five years after radiation. "Still hanging in there," I said and, with an attempt at humor, I added, "I could still be accused of rape if the woman helped me."

"Take Viagra," Dr. Mizrachi said. "I do."

I was surprised to hear him say this. "Your goals must be different than mine," I told him.

"Sure they are," he said. "But it's great for everybody, one of the greatest inventions of mankind."

I asked him about side effects I've heard of, that you feel like you're having a heart attack as it kicks in and also that there's the possibility that your erection won't go down and you might end up at the emergency room, an embarrassing possibility.

"No, not at all, doesn't happen." He wrote out a prescription and then told me about a small butcher shop near the Port Authority Terminal that had great veal at inexpensive prices. I pictured Dr. Mizrachi eating out at Italian restaurants or cooking great Italian meals at home, drinking good peasant wines and making it with several women every night, all of whom loved him.

We were around twenty-five years apart. Life changes, I thought. When I was younger I could have used a pill to keep my pecker down. Now I needed one to keep it up, though I'd sooner settle for warm cuddling every night than the acrobatic sex I imagine Dr. Mizrachi engages in.

I wished him a wonderful trip and we shook hands.

"See you in four months," he said. "Treat yourself well."

I made an appointment with Sandra for March and walked out into the sunshine toward 12th Street—a warm spring-like day, even though it was mid-November. I was free until the evening, when my son and daughter-in-law were taking me to a wine-tasting class, the first I've ever been to. I was sure Dr. Mizrachi would approve.

My Geisha Barber

I first met Seiko when I went with my wife and daughter for a shiatsu massage in the basement of Hoshi Coupe, a stylish hair salon owned by a Japanese woman near where we live on the Upper West Side. Outside the sign reads Hoshi Coupe, New York and Paris, a somewhat incongruous pairing given grungy Broadway at 108th Street, but the interior of Hoshi Coupe does have a sort of Soho stark look that suggests a European sensibility. My wife gave the family this present for Father's Day, and she went downstairs for the first massage.

While my daughter and I were sitting and waiting, one of the haircutters started talking to me and kept running her hands through my hair. "I give you good haircut," she said in a heavy Japanese accent. "I like silver color." She continued running her hands thru my scalp. My twelve-year-old daughter was aghast at her familiarity, but I was flattered. My hair is thin, and I am always uneasy when I get a haircut. Over the years I have found barbers I like, but then they move to other shops or else I sense they are tired of cutting my hair and rush through and I end up going somewhere else. The woman gave me her card. I said I would call the next time I needed a haircut.

I have been using Seiko for five years now, the longest I have ever been to one barber. I like women doing personal things for me, like cutting my hair or giving me a massage. One year I allowed myself the luxury of going to a female trainer at a gym and got in the best shape of my life until she left to attend graduate school and I stopped going.

Seiko is around five foot one and probably in her early fifties, but she looks younger. She has thin, taut lines in her face and neck, and wears glasses with large, fashionable rims, black stylish blouses, big earrings and jewelry, and high shoes or sneakers that add three or four inches to her height. I like the way she concentrates when she cuts my hair. She spends at least forty-five minutes as she carefully and elaborately makes each side even with the other. Other barbers have cut my hair in less than ten minutes, looking bored the whole time, but Seiko takes me seriously. Over the years I have become familiar with her. After all, we spend nearly an hour at a time together. She snorts slightly as she breathes. One nostril seems blocked, perhaps allergies or a deviated septum. She likes to talk, though often I don't understand her or she misunderstands me. We communicate in a sort of pidgin English.

"You go Bear Mountain this summer?" she asks.

"Vermont," I say. "I go Vermont."

"Right," she says, but I know the next time she will ask about Bear Mountain again.

Sometimes she brushes against me as she leans over to cut my hair. I shift my knees, but I enjoy the slight pressure of her body. She can't weigh more than one hundred pounds, but she is wiry and straight and moves with swiftness and energy.

I ask her about Japan's prime minister, hoping to impress her with my knowledge of her country, though she seems more interested in American culture than her own.

"I heard he just got divorced," I say, "and his girlfriend committed suicide when he wouldn't marry her." I have read in a newspaper that the girlfriend was a geisha, though I'm not exactly sure what a geisha is, whether that means she is a high class prostitute or just a woman who specializes in entertaining men in restaurants and clubs.

"In Japan there is saying, successful men need more than one woman," Seiko says.

"Yes, like Mr. Clinton," I answer.

Seiko laughs. "But not Mr. Bush," she says. "Not great enough."

This is the first time we have ever discussed politics. I wonder if Seiko is a liberal.

"You have girlfriends?" Seiko asks. I am flattered by her question. Is she flirting? She knows I am married and have a daughter. Or does she think I'm successful and therefore deserve one? She does have a kind of flirtiness about her. Most of her customers are men. There is a forwardness about her, combined with an Asian delicacy, that I find appealing. She is a sort of geisha-barber, but she is also a shrewd businesswoman. I leave large tips and I imagine her other male customers do too.

"No, no girlfriends," I say.

"Too quiet," she says.

When the haircut is finished and I have paid, she shakes my hand and kisses me on the cheek.

I think of her that afternoon and then again at night after my wife is asleep, and I remember the sound of Seiko's labored breathing. But by the next morning I forget about her and rarely think of her again until two months later when I need another haircut and call for an appointment.

The American Dream

During her fall break from college, Amelia and I watched a politician on TV talk about making the American Dream come true for all Americans. Amelia snorted. "When I hear the words American Dream, I want to vomit," she said.

"People do come here for opportunity," I said. "At least their children can become doctors."

"Not if you're black," she said.

I told her I thought it was more about class than race.

Amelia had tears in her eyes as she insisted on the inequity of American life, even though I tried to explain that I didn't disagree with her.

Later she came back into the living room and lay down on the sofa next to me. "I get so frustrated when I argue," she said. "I know what I believe, but I can't say it clearly."

She is always so argumentative with me that I feel attacked, but I also see that she is trying out ideas.

Once, shopping at the food co-op in Brattleboro, Vermont, where we vacation in the summer, Amelia said eating well is a privilege that makes her feel guilty. "Yes, it is," I answered. I wanted to tell her that everything is a privilege—going to college, listening to a CD, hailing a cab. The goal is to maintain a balance about the inequities in life—doing something about it, but also keeping the ability to enjoy yourself. If guilt helps you do things to help others, that's fine, but it can be a terrible thing when overdone. I said nothing of this, though, not wanting to appear critical.

Amelia also told me that we should buy big boxes of raisins and not the little packets that we have at home, because the small boxes waste paper. I told her I'd speak to her mother about it. But when I thought about it I realized that the small boxes serve a purpose. I limit myself to one at a time. With the big boxes I eat much more. So I moved the small packets of raisins to the back of the cupboard, out of sight.

Flying To Minnesota

Up at 4:35 AM for an eight o'clock flight to visit Amelia at Macalester College in St. Paul. Have to be at airport at six. You know it's early when the *New York Times* hasn't been delivered yet.

Take thyroid pill, shower, get dressed. Pour health food cereal into bowl with soy milk. (I am my mother's son and overly careful of what I eat.)

Alice is up and makes coffee. I hear the paper land at the back door. My wife, the news junky, grabs the first section. I read one headline: "FBI Issues Alert of New Terror" and underneath in smaller letters, "No Specifics Given." Not very promising for someone who doesn't like to fly to begin with. The cab service calls fifteen minutes early to say the driver's downstairs. I finish packing and squeeze in the dozen bagels Amelia has requested. She's got our schedule planned. Meet one-fifteen at the Student Center, lunch at the health food store off campus and shop for health food for her room (she's her father's daughter), watch her in jayvee soccer game, then a trip to the world's largest shopping mall to buy her a winter coat. Be nice to meet some of her friends from soccer. Some of them are older and live off campus where Amelia, who's a freshman, tells us she spends much of her time, which worries me, but I have to remember that she's on her own now, except for the bagels.

We're late getting downstairs and the driver is impatient. Wants to get out to the airport and back. Traffic is light and we reach LaGuardia in twenty minutes. I give the driver a big tip as a form of apology for keeping him waiting. (I'm also my father's son. He was a big tipper and always picked up the tab in a restaurant.)

The airport is nearly empty. Two National Guardsmen stand near the entrance in camouflage uniforms. They are so still I think at first they are manikins. Everybody loves people in uniforms now. In the Sixties and Seventies I remember firemen getting bricks hurled at them when they drove to fires in poor neighborhoods.

Early morning sunlight comes pouring through the terminal as we wait on line to board. Airline officials stop a kindly looking old woman ahead of us and make her step aside. They go over her body carefully with a detector. Right behind us is an Orthodox rabbi, a small middle-aged man with a black fedora and a beard. He is also searched. Maybe the most innocuous-looking ones are the most suspect, though I'd probably be pretty nervous if I was seated between two men in turbans.

The plane is less than half filled. Northwest must be taking a bath on this flight. The rabbi's in the section ahead of us. When a woman sits next to him, he moves to a seat further back. A few minutes later he moves back to our section in an empty row and sits near the window. He is carrying a half-eaten banana and an apple. I'm not religious, and have never cared for most rabbis. When Alice and I were married, we had a religious ceremony with Rabbi Chuck, whom I heard of through a friend at the American Civil Liberties Union. When I told Rabbi Chuck I didn't believe in God, he said it wasn't necessary to mention Him in the ceremony. I was so impressed I told him he could if he wanted to. Rabbi Chuck incorporated an American Indian love poem into the ceremony, but—so as not to offend any family members— didn't mention its origin. Eventually he quit the rabbinate and became the director of a Jewish activist group that tried to promote peace between Jews and Arabs.

The Orthodox rabbi takes off his fedora and wraps the phylactery around his head. The small black box looks a little like a party hat. I admire the rabbi for praying in public. I am always embarrassed at sticking out, and find it hard even to take notes on a plane as I am doing now, not wanting to appear pretentious. After some initial bumpiness the flight has grown smoother. I feel safe with the rabbi nearby.

Alice has moved to the seat in front of me so she can spread out as she does the crossword puzzle, and I whisper flirtatiously to her between the seats and ask her for her phone number.

As we approach the airport in Minneapolis the sun comes out from behind an overcast sky, bathing the cabin in sunlight.

All at once I remember sunny bright days years ago back in the Heights, and the old ladies in long dresses and hats who used to sit in wooden fold-up chairs along Fort Washington Avenue, facing the P.S. 187 schoolyard. I would pass them on my way home for a glass of milk, before rushing back to the schoolyard to play until it got dark. Now they're all dead and I'm on the verge of becoming an old man.